FIC GEN
Manoa, J.
Talk to me
3090020501039   8/2/16

THE ONE

Talk to Me

j. manoa

EPIC
Press

Talk to Me
The One: Book #2

Written by J. Manoa

Copyright © 2016 by Abdo Consulting Group, Inc.

Published by EPIC Press™
PO Box 398166
Minneapolis, MN 55439

Cover design by Candice Keimig
Images for cover art obtained from iStockPhoto.com
Edited by Ryan Hume

LIBRARY OF CONGRESS CATALOGING-IN-PUBLICATION DATA

Manoa, J.
Talk to me / J. Manoa.
p. cm. — (The one; #2)
Summary: Resentful that he is being limited, Odin begins to rebel against the authorities at school and home. Odin becomes suspicious that his parents aren't the loving caregivers they claim to be, but instead manipulative captors programming his every action and thought. When he finally learns the stark truth, that everything in his life up to this point has been a lie, he reaches a point of no return.
ISBN 978-1-68076-051-4 (hardcover)
1. Interpersonal relations—Fiction. 2. Family life—Fiction. 3. Behavior—Fiction.
4. Schools—Fiction. 5. Young adult fiction. I. Title.
[Fic]—dc23
2015949417

EPIC
Press

EPICPRESS.COM

To my mom, for everything

1

"**Y**OU'RE A SMART KID, ODIN," HE SAYS, LOOKING at me directly in the eyes. "I don't think I have to explain why I called you in here."

He leans forward with his elbows on the table. The dark circles under his eyes look like Halloween makeup he never washed off. The light bulb above him reflects through the thin hair pulled up and away from his forehead.

"So." He leans back with enough force that the springs of his chair groan with the effort. "How about you explain it to me? What's going on?"

I shrug. That's all the explanation he deserves.

Vice Principal Faria was a history teacher ten

years ago, and a beat cop ten years before that. He keeps his two citations for bravery in frames on the wall on either side of his master's degree. He attended night classes and later full-time following his honorable discharge from the Seattle Police Department, six months after he was sued for brutalizing an unarmed man whom he suspected was responsible for an armed robbery. The actual robber was arrested an hour later walking out of his apartment building, which happened to be the location of the robbery. Faria also stole cable and sold illegal fireworks, but no one took him to court for those.

"It's just funny that a kid like you can go through three years without an incident and then, three weeks before summer break, suddenly has every teacher complaining. So either something has changed in your behavior or teachers have been extremely lenient for far too long."

He's talking about the incident with Romero this morning during second period, when I told the class all the information about the book before Romero could. It was an experiment: What happens when one of his students gives credit for the research that Romero doesn't give credit for? The student gets sent to the office. All because I correctly added, "You got that from Wikipedia," to Romero's comment that J.D. Salinger wrote several other stories that were rewritten or never published, which included the character from *The Catcher in the Rye*. He got really angry when I started naming them: *I'm Crazy, This Sandwich Has No Mayonnaise, Are You Banging Your Head Against the Wall?* The last one was particularly fun. Romero's face was so red and his mouth sealed so tight that it looked like he was about to do exactly that. I even made sure to pitch my voice up so it came off as a question. Like, Mr. Romero, are you banging your head against the wall because a student is calling you on your bullshit?

Or maybe it was the little tiff Ms. Henderson had yesterday when I gave the answer to every question before she finished asking. Not my fault she's used the same example questions every year that she's been teaching. Maybe think of something new rather just reusing the same materials over and over again? But then, that would require having to do the same math she demands of her students. And that would be too much work.

"Well," Faria says after figuring out that I'm not interested in chatting, "if you don't want to explain what's going on, then we can sit here for a while. See if that gets the conversation rolling."

What I'm absolutely not sitting here for, in this tiny office with its bookshelves of unread adolescent psychology books and encyclopedia volumes used only for punishment, is the fight with Kevin. He spent a couple nights in the hospital, in the wing named after his great grandfather, and has been in and out for various treatments over the last month. His parents worked out a deal where his assignments are sent every night and he turns them in through email while he recovers at home. It's sad that he isn't here since his jaw is wired shut; that would make everyone in the school happy.

After the initial spread of rumors—everything from Kevin having such massive brain damage that he can now only move his left ring and right index fingers, to me picking up one of the concrete benches and smacking him with it like a baseball bat—the grapevine dried up. Talking behind someone's back is only fun when there's a back to talk behind. A few teachers heard hints about the fight but nothing more. Most of the blood near the benches washed away in that night's rain and the janitors cleaned the little that dropped in the hallway without question. The students are always really good at keeping certain things secret, like when a couple of other sophomores walked in on Jenny Robinson and some guy who graduated last year having sex in the science lab. None of the teachers heard about that. A couple of them asked Kevin what happened, but he gave them the same story he gave his parents—bike accident, backed up by all his friends. No one ever wants to admit they got their ass kicked. Especially by someone smaller and, he would say, weaker than him.

Fortunately Kevin's slander against Evelyn went nowhere. Not even Kevin's friends supported those.

"Is it something at home?" Faria asks, because he's far less comfortable with silence than I am. "Maybe that's it."

I look him dead in the eyes and say nothing. It's what he hates most. There's no chance of slipping up or establishing a rapport when the other person is silent. He uses the same tactic on us as he did with suspects. Says a lot about how he views his students.

Nothing has happened at home. Literally.

"Five complaints in just over two weeks," he says. "You gunning for some kind of record?" He looks down at the little yellow teacher complaint papers on his desk. "Tardiness, talking back, refusing to turn in assignments, more talking back." He fans them out in one hand. "Five of a kind. I'd be unbeatable in poker."

I scoff. "You'd also be cheating."

He grins. "Funny you should mention that." He thinks he got me. He has no idea who he's talking to. "Since you seem to have quit doing homework completely, a lot of your teachers are wondering how you also managed to get every single question right on every exam."

I shrug again—not like I don't know, more like I absolutely do know. I know everything.

He leans back in his chair, looks up at the ceiling and rubs his hands together. "You know what really gets me, Odin?"

I probably do, but I also know that you're going to tell me anyway.

"It isn't the students who don't do the work and then do badly. At least there's a reason for that. It's student like you who could so easily do the work. And who have, perfectly, for years, but just don't." He flips through another stack of papers on his desk, a bigger one of white sheets. "Your evaluations all say the same thing: bright, smart, tons of potential. That's actually written here." He holds the paper up for me to see. It was Mrs. Davis, chemistry, last year. "'Tons,'" he repeats for emphasis, "of potential. You're a smart kid, I'm sure you know exactly what a ton is."

This makes me chuckle.

"Is something funny?"

I shake my head.

"So you disrupt the lesson, quit doing the work necessary to understand the lesson, and yet you've had four exams recently and not gotten a single answer wrong." He rocks back and forth in his chair. "I'm not saying you *are* cheating but I am saying that for most other students, this would look like cheating."

I continue to say nothing.

He lets out one loud breath. "Usually this is the point where you try to defend yourself."

"I don't have to," I say.

He tilts his head from a lack of comprehension, like a dog hearing a new sound.

"Why would I cheat when I can know every answer without even trying?"

He sticks out his bottom lip and nods, trying to look both impressed and condescending.

"What's funny to me then," he says, "is that a smart kid like you would be content with settling for B's when you could be easily getting A's. Especially after three years of working so hard to keep your GPA high. It's almost a shame to see it all wasted."

"Wasted?" I say. I wait to continue, letting the word linger like an odor. "Wasted is all the time I spend doing unnecessary busywork for classes so easy I could sleep through them, and still answer every question correctly. So why should I waste my time when there are more interesting, more important things to spend it on?"

"Like what?" he says.

"If you don't know then I'm not going to tell you."

He scowls. His nostrils flare. He looks away with a huff.

"Look, son," he starts.

"Don't call me that."

"Look, *boy*," he begins again, "I don't know what's caused this sudden attitude and frankly I don't give a shit." He makes sure to emphasize that word as though a school authority swearing is supposed to frighten me. "All I know is that teachers are complaining about your conduct and you're disturbing classes."

"That's not my problem."

"You're right, it's my problem, and here's how we're going to fix it." He leans onto the desk, bringing his wide shoulders forward. They're each almost the size of his head. It's an obvious attempt at intimidation. "First of all, I'm calling your parents in for a conference. Second, for the next week instead of going to class you'll be coming here, to the office, and doing your work under my supervision. Third, if you don't give up this whole anti-homework protest or rebellion or whatever childish shit you're pulling, then once this year is over we—meaning you, me, your parents, and Principal Hauser—are going to have a discussion about whether or not you'll be welcome at this school next year." He keeps his eyes fixed to mine. "*Now* it's your problem."

Knowing what's coming next, I can't help but smile.

"Something still funny?" he asks.

"Not yet," I say.

He points at the door. "We're done here."

I don't move.

He picks up his phone receiver and dials one number. "Cathy," he says to the office receptionist outside, "get me the number for Odin Lewis's parents—"

I reach over and hold down the button to disconnect his call. I can see why this action is such a cliché. It feels awesome.

The scowl and flared nostrils again. He'd punch me, if not for the lawsuit he fears would follow.

"Daryl Corker," I say.

He glares at me.

"I think Principal Hauser would be surprised to know why a respected teacher would suddenly leave town instead of taking the promotion he clearly wanted."

"I have no idea what you're talking about."

"Really?" I say with all the fake surprise I can muster. "You don't remember? Ten years ago, you and Mr. Corker were both up for this job. You knew you didn't have a chance because Hauser didn't like you very much—hard to understand why not—while he and Corker were old friends and even helped each other get started in teaching." Faria's expression freezes, nothing. Now he'd be good at poker. "So you used some of your remaining police connections to dig through Corker's files and found that in 1973, long before Corker even considered being a teacher, he was arrested on felony marijuana cultivation of fewer than fifty plants, punishable by up to five years in prison. His lawyer pleaded down to misdemeanor possession and Corker received a year of probation and two hundred hours of community service. Of course, this didn't stop you from convincing Corker that if the parent-teacher committee found out that the vice principal in charge of maintaining order at school was busted for drug dealing, your words, it would be the end of his career."

Faria's eyes are big and still. He's seen a ghost. One he thought long gone.

"Corker withdrew himself from consideration without explaining anything to Hauser, and you, being the only option left, received the job you have today."

He shakes his head, angry and disbelieving, but frightened into inaction.

"What happened to Mr. Corker anyway?"

Faria freezes again.

"You know," I say, sympathetically, "it's not your fault he killed himself."

His chest rises and falls with heavy breath, he's even shaking slightly.

"You couldn't have known that he'd previously been treated for depression, or that he'd be completely unable to find work and his wife would leave him. You also couldn't have known that Hauser would be so distraught over his friend's death that he'd actually request a two-month-long leave of absence during which you acted as principal and solidified yourself both in this job and as Hauser's successor upon his retirement. You just knew there was a job you wanted and you couldn't stand the idea of anyone getting in your way for it."

He says nothing.

"Man," I say, shaking my head, "you are cutthroat."

Still nothing.

"So here's what we're gonna do," I say, hoping that in his quietly swelling rage and fear he appreciates the parallel. "First, I'm not going to receive any kind of punishment. No calls. No coming to the office. Nothing. Second, you're not going to tell anyone anything about the conversation we had here today. And third, well . . . I don't really have a third, so you can just use your imagination on that one."

He exhales a grunt and looks away. He knows he's beaten and he hates it. "How do you know any of this?" he asks.

"Because I know everything," I say. "And I'm tired of limiting myself to make you and people like you happy."

He remains turned away and silent.

"Are we finished?"

Frozen.

"Okay, let me rephrase that, we are finished." I push my seat back and stand. He's shrunken in his chair, hunched over and broken. "Just remember, for anything you say about me, there are a dozen things I will say about you. And this school loves to talk."

He shakes his head helplessly.

"Don't forget to take one of your carvedilol pills. You don't wanna have a heart attack."

I leave the door open on my way out.

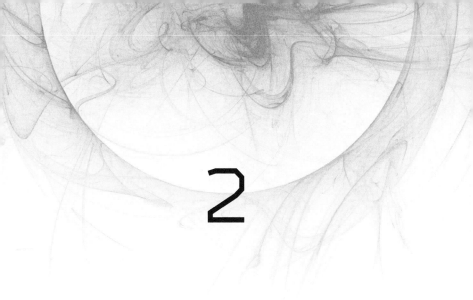

2

IFOLD OVER MYSELF FOR A BETTER LOOK. THE FOUR corners of the bed finally seem level with each other and the whole thing floats there high enough that I could slide underneath it, if I weren't afraid that I might lose control and drop it onto myself.

Excellent.

"Heaviest one yet. Now just have to keep it from falling."

I lower my hand slowly toward the floor while imagining the bed doing the same. It stutters on the way down, fast, then stopping, then slow, then fast. The descent feels like it takes minutes but only lasts a few seconds. I stop it an inch off the floor.

I let the bed hover as I breathe in and out deeply. I picture the bed dropping very gently with each angle settling into the grooves of the carpet. One corner lowers into the groove from a decade of sitting in one place. The far corner is next. Only the foot of the bed remains an inch above the floor. I stretch around to see that corners are lined up before lowering the remaining half of the bed down. It settles into the carpet with a muffled rustle.

Very good.

"It's not that hard, actually. Seems like surface area is less important than just the shape of it, the number of different planes and points of articulation. Like a car would probably be easier than a person."

Would be simple to find out.

"No."

There's the now familiar mental jolt of Wendell's laughter.

It would be an impressive feat.

"No. This stuff is one thing," I say, gesturing at the furniture and books around me, the things I've used to practice with for the last month. Only two things left to try: the desk with my computer still on it and the fully loaded bookshelf. I'm still too shaky on lifting and lowering to try objects that have other objects that may fall off. "But anything happens to the car and I'll be in some serious shit with Ben and Aida."

You also appear to be getting better at avoiding trouble.

"Yeah," I say quietly. I'll admit, it felt pretty badass talking to Faria like that. I'm sure hundreds of my fellow students would love to do the exact same thing. But now, I can't help feeling a little remorseful. Not because he was trying to bust me—that part was necessary—but I might've gone a little too far.

It is what needed to be done.

I know Wendell can't hear my thoughts, only

what I actually say, but sometimes he does seem to know a bit more than I'd like him to. "It was pretty harsh, though. Maybe a bit too dark."

No. Never apologize for doing what is necessary. Save your excuses for the necessary things you have yet to do.

He means my friends, family, or what is called my family, school, everything that's made up the bulk of my life thus far. He's labeled them distractions specifically designed to keep me from reaching my full potential, whatever that potential may be. He's never been clear on that, and since I can't exactly talk about this with anyone else, what I'm left with are such vague and cryptic statements as "necessary things you have yet to do." At least he's learned to keep such chatter to when no one else is around. It's better for keeping a low profile than pushing for a response when others could hear.

These are all important steps.

"Yeah, but steps toward what?"

Toward order.

That's another of his favorite terms lately: order.

All progress requires a first step, and that first step is always the hardest. It is the most uncertain and doubtful. But every subsequent step becomes that much easier.

I look at the room around me, the bed I remember from my first day in this house, the years of books on the shelf, the poster, the comics I stopped collecting long ago, the old toys in the closet that I've outgrown and haven't played with in forever but just can't get rid of. The sum total of my life. All of which, it seems, I'll have to give up one day.

This Faria, he is nothing, but he is a first step. Your interaction is not about him, it is about what he represents.

"And what is that?" I ask, more for confirmation than clarity.

Those who wish to limit you. And there are many. They are afraid because they know you are stronger than they are. It means they will no longer have control. Their order will no longer apply.

I sigh. It's the same thing every time. Order and control. Fear and limits. It's as though he, or I, maybe, can't think of anything new or specific to say. Instead, he continues using the same terms over and over. Maybe even he can't grasp the bigness of the situation he describes any more than I can. How can I? My life has been in this room, in this house, at school, around this town. I've known little else and remember nearly nothing. All I know is my experience. A single person has no concept of a million. One can't comprehend infinity even when surrounded by it.

Faria is unimportant as anything other than a symbol. Dealing with him makes it easier to deal with the rest of them.

Them, another of his favorites. A favorite of many people, really. Other students, newscasters, online conspiracy theorists, anyone looking for a nebulous, mysterious threat to divide themselves from. Us and them. Doesn't matter who *they* are, only matters that *they* are not *us*. The scope of my experiences might be tiny, but at least *they* have a face. It could be Kevin and his former cronies, Henderson, Faria, maybe even Aida and Ben. Real people that I can see and know exist. Not some group of nameless, imagined villains created solely to make me, *us*, feel like we're just. *We* are right. *They* are wrong. That's all we need to know.

What is important is not what came before, but what comes next.

I shake my head in dismissal. I lower into position again, eyes level to the plane where the mattress emerges from the bed frame. The next step, I imagine, is getting them both into the air and then separated one from the other. That should be pretty cool.

I begin the movement the same way as before, picturing the entire bed lifting from the ground. I raise my open hand in the way I want the bed to move. It does so. Lifting is the easy part; it's turning and manipulating while floating that's tricky. Compound movements. I almost broke my computer that way. When the bed frame reaches four inches off the floor, I hold that image in my mind while picturing the mattress inside the frame lifting up, moving on its own.

A single knock on the door snaps my concentration. Half of the bed falls to an inch off the ground before I catch it.

He's started doing that lately. Just one knock on the door to get my attention. It used to be one knock and "Dinner!" We don't even talk that much anymore.

This is how we live now.

Andre laughs loudly at an old episode of *The Simpsons* that he's seen a dozen times before. I've seen it at least as many. It's the *Flaming Moe* episode. Classic. I could probably recite several lines from memory, or all of them if I wanted.

Last week Aida and Ben—Mom and Dad as

I still call them to their faces—lifted their ban on the television being on during dinner. Andre immediately asked to change seats so he could keep his head tilted to the screen rather than straight at me. This means I have to spend my entire meal seated across from a woman who in some ways is less my mother than my captor. I can't even look at her without feeling my pulse rise. At least I've kept the silverware from doing the same.

Originally they thought not having the television on would promote conversation among the family. Then a few weeks of quiet made the dead air more pronounced. Silence can be louder than the noise it replaces. So, like most people, instead of improving on their failure, they decided to cover it up. Andre was happy, he got to enjoy the hour of *Simpsons* reruns that he'd been denied for years. I'm pretty sure no one else is happy with this arrangement. And they haven't been for a while.

"The wax never lies," Andre says before laughing again.

Mostly I hear the scrapes and taps of metal on ceramic. The sound of food being mashed between my teeth. Aida and Ben ask each other half-questions and receive half-answers, "Did you remember to call?" "Yes." "Okay. And the florist?" "Yes, I did." Tonight though, it's nothing but silence between them. Between all of us except for Andre and the television. He laughs again before saying something that ends with my name.

"What?" I reply.

"Remember that time you jinxed me and I couldn't talk until someone said my name?"

"I remember that," I say, unsure how else to respond.

He goes back to the show.

"Hon," Aida says, tapping the table in front of Andre. "How about you finish your dinner and then watch TV?"

"But this is the best part."

"If you know the show that well then you don't need to watch it again."

Andre huffs. "Fine." He cuts a giant piece of baked chicken and stuffs the whole thing in his mouth. His eyes go to the TV as he chews. I stare back at my own plate. Aida's sigh covers the sounds of Homer and Bart.

"So, Odin," she says. I take my own forkful. "How was school today?"

I feel the lack of expression on my face as I glance up at her. I chew slowly and make sure to swallow before answering. It gives the illusion of being polite.

"Fine."

"Anything new?"

"No."

"Not even with the year ending or anything?"

Andre's knife scrapes loudly as he takes another enormous bite. Ben continues eating as well, as unperturbed as ever.

"Not really."

"Okay," she says with a dismissive shrug.

I glance up from my plate just enough to see Aida and Ben exchange a look with each other. She shakes her head pathetically. I continue eating.

I wonder what they heard from Wiggins, or whoever their informant is. That I was called to the office? That Faria and I spoke? I guarantee Faria didn't reveal anything about our conversation. He's not that stupid. They, Aida and Ben, aren't nearly concerned enough to know what was said. Might've been one of the teachers acting on their own. I'll have to check on that tomorrow.

"Done," Andre says.

"World record," Ben says dryly.

"Can I go now?"

Aida points at the small pile of leftover peas and carrots sitting neglected on the side of the plate.

"I'm full," Andre says.

Aida says nothing.

"Go ahead," Ben says, motioning for Andre to go. "You can clean up after."

Andre pushes his seat back and immediately plops down on the couch, just as the show cuts to the first commercial break.

I keep Aida in mind first and the images flash. The last three days run backward, as if rewinding. The only people she'd interacted with outside of the family were charity representatives and Mrs. Aukerman next door when some of our mail was left in their box.

Ben is next. He hadn't spoken with anyone from the school either. There was someone else, a man I didn't recognize with spiky black hair and wearing a collared shirt and tie, whom Ben met two days ago at a coffee shop. He told Ben that I'd been having troubles at school. Acting out, talking back. He said nothing about Kevin. Their conversation—completed as instantly as a thought—offered no proof whether this man didn't know much or wasn't revealing everything.

I'm sure Ben mentioned the school trouble to Aida sometime that night. There's no need to peek at that. The quick glance back is enough to know what I'm dealing with.

My monitoring of them is no worse than what they do to me every day.

"Odin?" Aida says again.

I look up, doing nothing to hide my irritation.

"You sure everything's okay at school?"

She knows things are not okay, they both do, but she wants me to say it for myself. That's their way. Let me believe every idea, suspicion, action, is one I originated. Give me the illusion of choice and I'll follow their path without knowing it.

"Fine," I say, meeting her gaze. "Why? What have you heard?"

"Heard?" she says, doing a good job of faking surprise. "Nothing. Especially from you. That's why I asked."

"What about from him?" I say, pointing my fork towards Ben at the end of the table.

He places his empty palms out as though he's got nothing to hide. "Hey," he says, "I didn't say anything."

"Yeah," I say, "I'm sure you didn't."

Let it go.

"What's that supposed to mean?"

"I don't know," I say, "why don't *you* tell me what it means? That way you'll feel like you thought of it yourself."

Ben's eyes narrow with that one.

"You know, so you don't feel manipulated into thinking a certain way."

Stop.

"And everything can be entirely by your choice."

Stop. That is too much.

"That's how it works, isn't it?" I look back and forth between them. They wear conflicting expressions of silence: Aida shocked, Ben cold.

They cannot know.

"Funny, you give the illusion of choice because that's what *they* tell you do to."

You will ruin everything.

"How ironic."

I can't help flexing my jaw at them, the same way I did at Kevin that day at the benches. Aida looks around the room, a subconscious sign of distance and disbelief. She crosses one arm in front of her. Protection and enclosure. Ben fixes his eyes on me and doesn't move. Confidence, not a hint of fear. That's what he wants me to think. I actually wish I had that level of control. Must be his training, military or otherwise. I guess Aida never went through that.

"What else have they told you to do?" I can at least keep my voice level, remain seated, a mass of potential energy not yet spent on motion. "What else do you know?"

Aida is about to cry. Vulnerability. I stare directly at her. "What?" I say with more force.

"Odin," Ben says firmly. "We don't know what you're talking about."

I snap my gaze at him. "That's not what I heard," I say.

Do not say anything!

"Where is this coming from?" he says, faking concern.

"Give him the basis of an idea," I say from memory, their memory. "So he can form it himself." Aida is slightly rocking in her seat. "We can't force him to open up," I recall their conversation clearer than they ever could. "That would guarantee that he pulls away."

Stop!

"Odin." Ben's nose wrinkles as he speaks. "Stop right now."

"No!" By now I'm sure Andre is listening. It doesn't matter. These are the same people he has to deal with. At least I'll have some way out, whatever it is. He'll be with them as long as they all live. "I'm tired of being controlled and handled by you or anyone else. I don't need it and I don't need you."

Ben stares at me, pushing his shoulders out to

emphasis his width compared to mine. It's that animal instinct that still exists in all of us, a subconscious attempt at intimidation. Faria tried it. It didn't work for him either.

Aida finally slinks away from her seat. She strides into the living room where I'm sure she puts her hands on Andre's back and tries to get him to ignore what's happening.

I continue my stare. I feel the tension in my back teeth. Ben has both hands curled into fists in front of him. He can't help it. I'm in control now.

"Don't even try it," I say. "You have no idea."

The line of muscles tenses in his forearms. In truth, if he were to lash out at me, I'm not sure what I could do. At least not what I could do that wouldn't lead to permanent damage. His eyes draw down. The knife next to my plate lies flat, two inches off the table. I try to push it down with the back of my hand, so he knows I'm not reaching for it, but the knife doesn't move. I consciously force it to drop.

I push my chair back and stand. He does the same, keeping his head titled back so I can't help but look up at the base of his chin.

We stare at each other. He's trying everything he can to look frightening, flexing through every breath, flaring his nostrils, all the animalistic shit that's hardwired into our evolutionary coding. But he knows better. He knows there's nothing more he can do. They say animals are more afraid of us than we are of them. He should be.

"I'm done with you," I say as I walk past.

They were not supposed to know.

They're out there talking with Andre right now. The real conversation will take place in a couple of hours when he's in his room and they're alone. That's when they'll start.

They were supposed to think everything was normal.

Aida will probably yell, maybe cry a little. She'll talk about how she never wanted this responsibility and maybe it's time to stop.

If they suspect that you know about them, it could make our situation more difficult.

Ben will be calm and hope it'll rub off on her. He'll seek out a reason for my outburst, something general first then more individual. He'll reassure her that they've done everything right and, if necessary, there is always a backup plan. The "support" team that's only thirty seconds away.

You ruined everything.

I can wait to listen to this but I don't need to. It doesn't matter what they say or do anymore. No matter.

"I don't care."

You should. This is your life we are talking about.

"You're goddamn right it is!" I shout before remembering that they could also be right outside my door, listening to everything. I speak more quietly. "Mine. Mine alone. But it's never once felt that way. Either they've been manipulating me or you have. I'm fucking tired of it."

Because you know nothing.

"No, you know nothing!" Again too loud. "I don't need you. Everything that's happened is because of you so just fucking leave again."

You need me. You just do not know it yet.

"Fuck you!" Pretty sure the living room could hear that.

I can feel him there, deep in some recess of my mind. A place you never imagine as tangible until suddenly it is. There but silent. Everything is silent. Inside my head and out.

As you wish.

"Goddamn right."

Then he's gone. I don't know where, I don't know how, but I know he is.

3

I'VE BEEN DREADING THIS RIDE ALL NIGHT, ONCE I realized there was no way to avoid it. It actually hasn't been as bad as expected. There's a palpable tension in the car, but not an awkward or intense one. Neither Aida nor I have anything we must say, nor anything we particularly want to say. We just roll along as we always have for the fifteen minutes it takes to get from the house to my school. Ben and Andre probably have a lot more to talk about on their trip. For us, it's less like riding with a friend, or worse yet, a captor, than riding with a taxi driver. Quiet and obligatory. Nothing more than that. The car pulls up to the curb in front of the long path to the school entrance and I get out. No talk. No goodbye. Her job is done.

I keep my head down as I walk up the wide passage to the entrance. The expanse of flat grass and sparse trees placed far from the walkway make the junior benches visible during the entire approach to the entrance. I see Richard and David there along with a couple of others. I haven't spoken to Richard since the incident that happened at that exact spot over a month ago. Haven't spoken to David since the lunch room. I glance up as I get closer to the benches and catch Richard's eyes. I nod to him out of instinct more than friendship. He turns away. I cross the last seam in the concrete, where the benches sit on an extension on the right of the path. David gives me an unwelcoming look: Don't come any closer. I continue through the door, past the senior boys on their benches. They wait until I'm gone down the hall before the conversation starts.

Just inside the entrance is the chubby security guard and the long-haired janitor. Everyone noticed the security guards at the beginning of the year. Then we learned to ignore them. The janitors are always unnoticed. They're shadows, always there, rarely considered. Wish it could be like that for me some days, like today.

I rush past the students lining the main hall, the closed classroom doors, my locker, Evelyn's locker where I placed a note three weeks ago that was never answered, and move directly to Room 248, Henderson's calculus class, today's first period in the rotating schedule. I drop my bag to the floor next to the seat assigned to me the first day. The only seat I'll ever have in this class. I wait. No one other than Mrs. Henderson will enter until seconds before the morning bell signals that they should be in their seats. That's how it is now.

The announcement comes before Henderson finishes unpacking her materials for the lesson. "Odin Lewis," Ms. O'Hara, Principal Hauser's assistant, says over the loud speaker, "please report to the principal's office." None of my classmates look at me when my name is called. "Odin Lewis, please come to Principal Hauser's office immediately." I'm two feet from the door when the whispers start. I'm thirty feet away when Henderson shushes my classmates.

Principal Hauser is talking with Ms. O'Hara at her desk when I arrive.

"You wanted to see me?" I say.

He points to the open door of his office. "Right in there." He returns to his conversation before I can ask what any of this is about.

Hauser's office walls are decorated with a large black-and-white photo of the school when it first opened in the 1970s, his framed degrees, various "Of the Year" awards for teaching and administrating, and a window looking into the fenced-in area behind the building. His view is metal sheds and piping, probably for the air conditioning and heat, then a few trees in the grass field ending at the street which curves around campus. His bookshelf against the rear wall holds a copy of every single yearbook the school has produced. The file cabinet next to it still has contact information for students from ten years ago. The center of the office is dominated by an L-shaped, oak desk that was donated to Hauser by one of the school's wealthier alumni and the two red-cushioned wooden chairs in front of it. Behind that desk, hidden at first by the computer monitor on its corner, sits a man with short black hair and glasses. He peeks around the monitor as I cross the line from the gray tile of the assistant area and onto the blue tile of the office.

"Ah, Odin," he says in a mild voice. "Please close the door and have a seat."

I can't place it but I've seen him somewhere before. He has a squarish face, is in his early forties, and wears a black suit. He types at his phone, the click sounds repeating so quickly they nearly make one sustained tone. I put my bag onto the chair closest to the door and stand next to it. He flicks the button on the side of the phone and puts it face down on the desk in front of him. A piece of plastic sits just inside his ear. Its color was matched to someone else's skin.

"I'd rather stand," I say.

"Your choice," he says. "My name is Randall Choi. I'm an intelligence analyst for the United States Department of Homeland Security's Domestic Resources Development Initiative. Although you may already know that by now, am I right?"

I shake my head although it's immediately clear that this is the "Choi" whom Ben had previously mentioned.

"Hmm," he says, leaning back, "so you decided to come here without knowing what was happening. Interesting."

"Why is that interesting?"

"Because it shows that you still have some trust in your surroundings."

"Or it means I don't care who you are because nothing here means anything to me."

"That's also possible. Interesting either way. Are

you sure you don't want to sit? This could take a while."

I cross my arms in front of me. He leans back and looks at me straight on. He wants to show that he has nothing to hide.

"I'm sure you have a million questions, but if you don't mind, I'd like to address some issues first which may help answer some of those questions." He pauses just long enough for me to nod. "Your parents, or guardians if you prefer that term, are employees of the DRDI. Specifically what we call Project Solar Flare, a dedicated program within the larger Initiative. They have been entrusted with your care until you're old enough to do so yourself without being a danger to those around you."

I show no surprise.

"But again, I suspect you may already know this," he says with a confident nod. "They have not contacted me nor do they know that I have made contact with you or that I am in this location. In fact, only my direct supervisors know that I'm here today. I trust you can be similarly discreet about this meeting." He continues before I agree. "I believe so. We placed you into their care to offer you the best possible chance at a normal childhood. The DRDI performed thorough investigations into every available living situation and decided that this was the best and most likely to provide you with the happiest and most fulfilling experience."

He keeps his fingers intertwined in front of him and speaks clearly and evenly. Like a news anchor. Even down to the earpiece.

"There are many both in and out of the Initiative who would have preferred to keep you in a secure facility after the incident, but I and a handful of others argued that such a tactic could result in stunted social development, withdrawal, and anger, and ultimately rob you of the normal experiences of childhood and young adulthood. I personally argued that given how . . . special . . . you may prove to be in later life, you should be afforded the chance to be average for as long as possible. That may not sound appealing right now, but trust me, once you've spent years outside of what could be considered normal or average, you start to miss it."

He tries for a reassuring smile. The smile works, the reassurance doesn't.

"My concern, and why I have decided to take the risk of making contact with you today, is primarily for your safety." His rhythm is one of practiced delivery. "Most of us are still committed to allowing you some level of normalcy, but with recent events, from the fight here which placed Kevin Clark in the hospital and possibly compromised your secrecy with other students, to lashing out at teachers and classmates, there has been renewed debate as to whether or not you can be trusted to live on the outside. What we wish—"

"Stop," I say. He blinks quickly, like I'd jumped from the audience to interrupt his monologue. "You've been watching me." I know this but I want him to admit it.

"In a way, yes. Of course, your parents monitor

your behavior at home and guide your growth."
He goes right back into his rhythm. Doesn't miss a
beat. "We watch the public. We monitor the school
and the town for unusual happenings. We have no
interest in your daily activities, just that your actions
don't compromise our position or yours. Recently,
however, there has been a noticeable change in your
behavior. This change *is* starting to be noticed. This
notice has renewed the doubts of those who would
rather see you in custody than allowed to move
freely through the world. You are not the only one
whose actions are under constant scrutiny."

"This is free?" I say. "Being monitored wherever
I go? Having fake parents program me into acting
a specific way? That's *free*?"

"Compared to a secured facility under twenty-
four-hour watch by armed guards, yes."

I shake my head in disbelief but I remain calm.
If he can be even, so can I.

"That's exactly what we're looking at here, Odin.
I've been authorized by my superiors to speak to

you openly and frankly about what is at stake solely because we believe that you deserve better than captivity. However, if your recent behavior continues, your situation may be removed from our control and handed to others who will not be so . . ."

I allow him to find the correct word.

"Understanding."

"This is unbelievable," I mutter.

"Why would I have any reason to lie to someone who can so easily find the truth? If you still don't believe me, go ahead and look for yourself."

I do, quickly, more quickly than I ever have before. It's skimming through a text looking for one specific word.

I see Choi over the last five days, on telephones, on email, over coffee with Ben, in video chat, on a plane, in a helicopter, talking in a meeting with two other people in a small conference room. One man has a sharp face and the other has a small chin with a sloping neck. The first wears a military uniform and the other a dark suit, like Choi's. I only recognize Choi. This was four days ago, before the latest incidents at school.

The one in uniform argued that "the subject," I assume me, shouldn't be allowed to remain outside of their watch. Unpredictable, unreliable, he called me. The other man, with short gray hair parted down the middle, asked for Choi's opinion.

"We've come this far," he said. "Perhaps as far as we can with this current situation."

"Glad to hear it," said the one with three stars on his shoulders.

"All due respect, sir, I'm not referring to custody. Before taking such a drastic step as abducting the boy, we should offer him something else and see if it can pacify him."

The gray-haired man with no chin stands in front of them. A large flat-screen monitor is installed into the front wall of the room. On the table between them all is an audio speaker. "What offer?" the man asked.

"Well, the only reason we haven't had to take action sooner is because the boy, Odin, is still trusting enough to not seek out answers he could so easily find. It may be best for us to demonstrate a little trust of our own."

The general shook his head. "That's a mistake," his voice a striking baritone.

"Doctor," said Gray Hair, leaning toward the speaker at the center of the table. "Are you still there?"

"Yes," said a soft voice with a slight mechanical buzz. A woman.

"Your thoughts?"

"I agree that it's too late to proceed with the current plan. However, if our operatives have done their job, as Mr. Choi believes they have, then Odin should have the foundation enough to choose what he knows to be right." The general shook his head while listening. The voice over the speaker continued, "He's never acted like this before, but he's also never been able to manifest his powers like this before."

"Except once," the general interrupted.

"And it was decided then that he was young enough to remain in the dark. That he could be lied to. But he's not so young anymore. It may be time for the truth. It was always the plan anyway, we may just have to adjust our schedule."

"Can we do that?"

"It's inconvenient," said Choi, "but it can be done."

"Doctor?"

"We should believe in him, sir. It may be our only choice."

"How would you do this?" Gray Hair asked.

"We could make contact at—"

"Do you see?" Choi asks from behind Principal Hauser's desk, pulling me out of the past and into the present. "Now do you believe that I have nothing but your best interest at heart?"

"Could have been staged," I say. "An act knowing that you'd be here inviting me to see that exact set up."

"That's always a possibility."

I narrow my eyes at him.

"The doctor was right. It's too late to expect you to believe this fantasy any longer. We've spent years preparing for when you could be trusted with this information. Here it is."

Choi frequently enunciated his words incorrectly when he was a kid. He elongated syllables, misplaced stress, and pronounced silent letters. His third grade class teased him mercilessly any time no adults were there to hear their crude imitations. This caused him to become extremely quiet until his parents pushed him to join various public speaking clubs around their home in San Francisco. Talking became easier over the years, but he still prepares as much as possible before any planned conversation.

I feel my expression soften a little before making the effort to sharpen it again.

"We believe trust still means something to you."

I could use his previous shame to bludgeon, like I did with Faria. I could force him to reveal every other secret he has. But I don't want to. For some reason, I want to believe him. I wish for everything he says to be true. It would be so much easier if it were.

"You're still uncertain," he says. "In the interest of honesty, please, ask me anything you'd like."

I think for a second before deciding where to start. What's his game? What does "honesty" mean to him?

"The meeting you had five days ago," I say, "the three of you in a room."

"Are you referring to the gray-haired gentleman and the general?"

I nod.

"Those are two of my superiors. Director Clancy Braxton is the head of the Domestic Resources Development Initiative, while General Edward Delgado is our military consultant. The voice over the phone is Dr. Alice Burnett."

Memories flood of an office with board games, puzzles, and toys. Children's finger paintings stapled inside the door. Bookcases of thick tomes. White walls on three sides with a fourth wall of glass from ceiling to floor, the largest window I'd ever seen, overlooking the tiny city streets. I'd begin every weekend there, staring down, admiring how small those people were. Adults that towered over me looked like ants. We'd play board games and talk about school. Dr. Alice Burnett. The only person other than Kevin who knew about Wendell. The only one who didn't later use that knowledge to attack me.

"I believe you know her."

"Yes," I whisper.

"Is there anything else you'd like to know?"

The questions jam so quickly in my mind that

none can get through. Burnett was the one who urged me to stop dwelling on my parents, my real parents. She told me that Wendell was a subconscious reaction to the anger I felt over losing them. Said that holding onto those feelings would only cause me misery. She taught me how to live.

He corrects himself. "Anything that you wouldn't be able to find on your own if you so chose?"

He knows that eliminates almost any question that I would otherwise ask, except maybe one.

"My parents," I say. "My birth parents. What happened to them?"

"You killed them."

All the air is sucked from the room.

"It was an accident, but it's why you were entrusted to our care in the first place . . ." He continues speaking, but I hear none of it. Everything is shaking. I see the lines across my mother's forehead. My father yelling, throwing his hand out for her. There's the reflection in the gleaming grill of the vehicle as it approaches. " . . . So nothing like that would ever happen again."

"I d-don't—"

"Odin," Choi says, beckoning me to look at him. "I don't mean to be cruel, but what happened happened, and there is nothing you can do. You can't allow yourself to get stuck on things which are long over. As talented as you may be, you can't change the past."

He's obviously spoken to Burnett a lot. Does he know everything she does?

"We need to focus on the present," he says, "and how we can move into the future without jeopardizing everything we have worked for and you have earned."

"What has Dr. Burnett told you?"

"Not much," he says. "Doctor-patient confidentiality exists even in our agency. The general has had quite a few words with her about that."

I see the truck again, the metal gleaming through

the blood, a scuff at the bottom of my mother's heel.

"In fact," he says, "I'll tell you a secret." He slumps forward slightly. "No one really knows what you may be able to do. We have some ideas and theories, but no one is quite exact about it yet. That's the reason why we're hoping that when the time comes, you'll be willing to work with us. We can all learn a lot together."

He glances on the clock above the door. "I understand this is a lot to digest," he says, as if on cue, "but we shouldn't talk much longer. We don't want the school's administration to become suspicious."

I take a second to gather myself, pushing the distant images from my mind. I nod uneasily. If his plan was to throw me off, it's worked. There's no way it wouldn't have worked.

He shifts forward in the seat. "Here's the bottom line, Odin: If you want to remain free, you can't draw attention to yourself. Fights, showing off in class, these are things that cause people to talk and to ask questions. Not only could these questions cause a public panic, but they would place you in immediate, grave danger. There are those who would like nothing more than to use such talents for their own means, those who would view you as a threat, and others, like myself, Dr. Burnett, and your family, who want to offer you a choice in how you use them or if you use them at all."

Aida and Ben, Mom and Dad, even knowing what I am, the danger I pose, still agreed to take me in. They may not have had much of a choice, but they still did it. They've always supported me. They've never treated me like a fake son or an experiment. A "project." They made me theirs.

"We have fought very hard to offer you the freedom you have today," Choi says. "We would hate to see you lose that."

I feel the tinge of responsibility now. I imagine the shame that my parents would feel knowing that they'd failed in their task to raise me.

"We've all worked too hard to fail now."

I know I'm being manipulated again. I know it. He knows it. He says exactly what's needed to placate me. He's practiced it—the bastard—playing into the obligation and trust that Aida and Ben—my handlers—have drilled into my mind. He's using my conditioning. I know this. It still works. Dammit, it still works.

"Odin," he says with a jolt in his voice, "do you understand?"

"Yes," I say, exactly as he expects. "I understand."

"Do you really understand?"

"Yes," I say again more slowly.

"Are you absolutely sure?"

"Yes, goddammit!"

"Good," he says, pushing back in the chair. He stands up. "Then I expect we'll never have to speak about this subject again."

He walks around the desk and toward the door.

"Is that all?" I ask.

"Yes," he says. "That's all."

"What about my questions?"

He stops and tilts his head at me.

"If you really want to know the answers," he says, "you don't need to ask."

Choi opens the office door. He motions for me to leave. I pick up my bag and slowly approach the exit. Choi nods as I pass.

Hauser sits in the reception area like a student sent to the principal's office. His eyes shift away from me, as I imagine a guilty student's do upon seeing him. I'd find the irony funny if I were in the mood to find anything funny.

"How was it?" he asks.

"Umm," I say.

"A little overwhelming?" Hauser points at the door behind me.

" . . . Yeah."

"Don't worry about that." Hauser stands. He straightens out his tie. "M.I.T. wouldn't send a recruiter all the way out here if you weren't important."

4

YOU CANNOT POSSIBLY BELIEVE THEM.

He waited until the middle of Mr. Zeller's lesson to start talking again, where I wouldn't be able to respond without drawing the exact kind of attention I'd been warned not to. All I can do for now is sit here and listen.

This was always part of their plan. Keep you passive. Keep you quiet.

The more I try to ignore him, the louder his words become. As though they echo outwardly from my mind to the every ends of my fingers and toes. His . . . voice, I guess . . . has never been this way before. Never so forceful.

Keep you contained. Controlled. Scared.

He's usually like a whisper. Now, he's like a public announcement system piped directly into my head. He's a speaker in my skull. The vibration is almost painful.

They want to limit the way you act. The way you think.

Zeller draws something like a twenty-legged Spiderman symbol on the board. He sounds like he's talking in another room down the hall. He says something about the electric field of a positive electrical charge over a metal surface.

While I want you to see the possibilities.

The words, the ones in my mind, dampen those around me. My every thought amplifies his voice. My own doubts and uncertainties, all the things I wish I had asked of this Choi guy before our sudden end, shout back to me.

Trust. You cannot trust them.

It only makes the feeling that much more intense.

They were afraid you had gotten too close. They changed their lie to keep lying.

I should have made him sit there, maybe pushed him into place until I checked every second of his story. Choi's whole existence from his first word to the second before I walked into that office.

They have done nothing but lie to you. Lie to you your whole life. Lie about your whole life.

I could have backed the desk against him until he could barely breathe. Lifted him up to the ceiling, upside down, and let all the blood rush to his head. I should have shaken him literally the way he shook me figuratively. Then I would have seen what he really is. The scared little kid with the speech problem. He would spill everything.

They have done nothing but limit you. Taught you to limit yourself. Talking of trust and obligation to cover themselves. Ingraining it into your mind.

I could have done so much more. I should have done so much more.

And now they are feeding off those limits.

I can still do it now if I want. Search through his history. Listen to every conversation he's ever had with Burnett or the others. Already too late to do any good. He's gone and now I know they've been watching me. They could do anything.

Lying about your parents.

Anything at all.

Blaming their deaths on you. A child. A loving child. For something so monstrous.

The truck. The blood.

They taught you not to look back on that time. Made it too painful to even imagine.

That's all I ever see.

Repeated it over and over until you believed them.

I never see what was around me. Around us. I never see the driver of the truck.

They took away your past. Replaced it with their own ideas.

They, my real parents, could have been pushed into the road.

They think that if they can control that most tragic time, they can control anything.

I remember a noise, I always thought it was a horn. It could have been a shot. A pistol from behind me. The building there. It was old with a face of stone and glass.

Repeated over and over. Reinforced. Until your life, your mind, was theirs.

Mom could have lost balance after the shot, fallen into the road as Dad reached to cover her. There was another noise. Louder than the first. Closer.

So that they could own you. Train you. Make you think and act exactly as they want you to.

No. It wasn't that. The noise was something else. A scream. She was scared.

Make it seem like it is your idea when they have been there, pushing it on you, for years. Repeating their lies until the truth no longer exists.

I can feel my fingers twitch. There's a coldness in

my hands. It's like winter has started in my veins. I grip my pen in one hand and clamp to the desk with the other until my arms go numb. I don't want to live this. Not again. Not ever again.

But that is why I am here. You do not have to listen to the lies anymore. You do not have to believe them. You do not have to buy into the reality they've created to keep you within their power.

"Odin?"

You can see outside of their walls. You can break through.

"Odin!"

Zeller is leaned toward me from the aisle between the desks in the first row. The eyes of every student point in my direction. Anne and the other suck-ups are turned as an audience. Miles has been pulled away from his drawing. Even Evelyn looks on, until I glance over to her.

Zeller walks back around his desk and points to another picture on the board: a single small circle on the blank field of the chalkboard.

"Odin, for a positive charge, in which direction do the field lines move?"

I rub my hands together. They are steady and warm. My pulse is barely above normal. I feel it in the thumb against my palm.

"Perhaps if you spent less time daydreaming," Zeller says, "and more time listening you would know that the class is on page two thirty-five in the text and not page two thirty-one, as you are."

I turn the pages quickly. The words are blurs.

"Can anyone else answer this very simple question?"

I see it all.

"Electric field lines accelerate away from a positive charge and toward a negative charge," I say. "As the field accelerates in all directions at once, there is an infinite number of lines which can be drawn from the charge. The number of lines drawn typically reflects the power of the charge."

Zeller's arms drop to his sides.

"Further, the fields of two positive charges on

the same plain do not overlap but instead push each other away from their points of origin in a pattern fitting with the power of each individual charge."

Zeller looks away for a moment before turning back to the board.

"Very good," he says, quietly to the chalk.

I feel my mouth curve upward, then the surge of Wendell's laugh.

Peons. Unimportant and insignificant. Their charade is falling.

At least here I still have some level of control.

The room always clears out fastest on days when the period immediately precedes lunch. Even the suck-ups hurry out the door. I unload several books to make room for my physics text. Shifting books assures that everyone else is gone before me.

Zeller moves toward the door with his books tucked under his arm. I say nothing and keep my head down toward my bag, as though I'm trying to find room for all the stuff I have to carry every day, all twenty pounds of it. To others it may look like I'm reloading my weapon. I hear Zeller's footsteps stop at the exit.

"Close the door when you leave," he says. His footsteps resume. I hear the door close.

"I thought you said you were leaving," I say as though there were someone around to hear me.

I cannot. Not while they are still trying to fill your head with their lies.

I easily slide the books into the bag. "They're not the ones in my head."

But they are. They have been there from the start. They own your thoughts. That was their plan.

After zipping the bag shut, I check out the window through the classroom door to see if anyone is there. All clear. "So have you. You came along at the same time."

I pull the backpack onto the seat of my desk. I look around at the room. Marie Curie reminds me, "Nothing in life is to be feared, it is only to be understood. Now is the time to understand more, so that we may fear less." Marie Curie also died in 1934 of aplastic anemia likely caused by prolonged exposure to the radioactive elements she discovered. She didn't live long enough to see her work in use as the atomic bomb.

"Why should I believe you?" I asked of Wendell, although it could also have been of Madame Curie.

Because I am the only one who tells you the truth.

I walk around to between the first row of chairs and the teacher's desk. I look out the window again, down the hall as far as I can. A couple of students wander slowly but otherwise nothing is in sight. "You're also the only one I can't check on."

Does that not mean something?

I step away from the door and lean onto the teacher's desk. This is what it must look like for Mr. Zeller at times, a class full of empty chairs, even when the students are there. "I don't know what to think anymore."

That means they have won. Project Solar Flare. They have you.

"No, they don't."

They have taken your desire to find the answers for yourself because you are afraid of what you may find.

I shake my head. Can he see the motion? When I look back on people, it's like a camera moving around the scene, but I'm not actually in their minds talking to them. I'm on the outside looking in. He's just the opposite. Does he then see what I see? When I shake my head, does his view shake? "It's not that."

What is it then?

"It's like there's something blocking me out. Anytime I get close to that moment, to what happened before my mother fell into the road, something forces me out. I can see . . ." I look back as far as I can. My first day of life: the hospital lights blurring through a plastic covering. My first day of school:

the other tiny children walking clumsily in the shoes their parents bought them to grow into. My first ice cream cone: chocolate and already melting before I wrapped it in my little hands. My mother, with her dark eyes and high forehead, hair bursting out like an explosion. My father, a shadow of stubble around his chin, lines at the corners of his eyes, flat nose, slight swelling of his ears. "I can see everything," I say. He was a boxer. I remember that now. He liked to tell me stories while we ate our ice cream. "Everything except that."

I see through the open door of the building to the sidewalk and the wide street behind it. It's an apartment building with metal mailboxes against one wall and a drawer for garbage on the other. There's metal scaffolding on the building across the road. Pedestrians walk in shorts and tank tops. It's a hot day. I hear a voice calling out to us. I move toward the door slowly. And that's it. A black space. Then comes the confusion, the desperation, the blood.

They have taught you to block it out. They have

twisted your memory so much that your mind is incapable of differentiating fiction from reality.

"No, they haven't," I say. There's Dr. Burnett seated in her brown leather chair across from me on a matching couch. I'm so high, my feet don't touch the ground. There's a Chinese checkers board between us. She plays yellow and I play green. We always choose those colors. She tells me that I shouldn't think about the bad things but I shouldn't be afraid of them either. They will only make me sad or angry. Sad because of what happened. Angry because I can't change it.

They claimed your life for themselves. They have turned your memory against you.

She says I can do anything except change the past.

That is how it began.

"It was an accident," I say. "I know it was. That's all there is to it."

Keep believing that, exactly as they told you.

"You tell me you're here to help—"

I cannot if you will not let me.

"—But all you've done is ruin everything. My family, my friends, my school, everything!"

Those are not important.

"Everyone hates me because of you. Because of what you've been telling me."

The more they fear you, the more they will hate you.

"And you won't leave me alone."

You must use their fe—

"Get out of my fucking head!"

The words echo through the empty class.

I breathe in and out a few times. A burning feeling swells in the back of my throat and spreads outward until my entire windpipe is on fire. I didn't even notice that I'm shaking, everywhere, as though the room were a freezer. The lines of desks in front of me pull to the left. There are already students gathering under the trees in the grass outside the windows. They don't see me here. Or they have and aren't looking now. I close my eyes and swallow, hard and dry, cringing through the motion. I steady myself until the shaking stops. All is still. Calm. I know he's gone.

I walk back to take the bag from my seat. The desk almost falls forward as I push down to lift my backpack from the chair. The classroom door remains closed. I look over the desks, mine, those in the front where the suck-ups sits, Denise behind me, and then Evelyn's seat back and to the right. I used to think it would be nice if we had been placed closer together. I don't think so anymore. Maybe it's best that she stays away.

I place both bag straps onto my shoulders and start toward the door. There's a motion through the classroom window, someone starting to move. They were probably coming to see what the noise was, only to find me, the troublemaker, yelling in an empty room. Stupid thing to do, but not something that would get me punished. I look out to see if anyone is visible through the window before opening the door.

They're on me as I step out. Eric and Dylan. Kevin's boys. Like they were waiting for me to leave.

Eric in front of me. Dylan behind me. All I see is Eric's nose, blackheads on the tip and grease around the nostrils.

"Think you're a tough guy now?" Eric says.

I look to the floor.

"That's right. Look away."

"Freak boy," says Dylan, his words hot on the back of my head. "Fucking talking to your pretend friend again, fucking freak?"

"What's wrong?" Eric's warm and stale breath right into my eyes. "No room to throw your shit around? No teachers to run to?"

They smell like cigarettes and dried sweat.

"I don't care what everyone says, I saw what happened. Had to swing books because you're too much of a fucking coward to use your fists like a fucking man."

"Yeah. Fucking coward."

One of Eric's shoes is about to come untied.

"You know he's gotta get surgery to fix his nose? Probably his jaw too."

The classroom door is just two feet away. Maybe I can make it there.

"Fucking pussy can't even look at me," Eric says. His head tilts side-to-side as he talks. The shadow of his nose shifts.

"Pussy," says Dylan.

"He spent three days in the hospital because of you throwing your little bag around." He laughs. "I thought only women fought with handbags."

Dylan laughs too.

I lock my jaw and look up. I stare directly into the center of Eric's eyes, two inches higher than my own.

"That's not my problem."

"It is now. You know why?"

His left eyeball has a red spot near the outer edge where he got poked by a toothpick as a kid. I never heard how it happened.

"Because he told us you were his. But now he's not here to stop us from whipping your little freak boy ass for fucking up our boy."

"We'll fuck you up," says Dylan.

"Everyone saying that Kevin's a bitch because of what you did. That Odin's this scary fucking monster—"

"I'm not a monster!" I yell before regretting it.

"That's fucking right you aren't. Just a scared little pussy."

Eric exhales directly onto my nose.

"And what're you gonna do, huh? Your little thrown bag shit isn't gonna work anymore. You got no backup. No one likes you. Even the teachers don't give a fuck about you."

"No one but your pretend friend," Dylan says.

Eric presses his forehead to mine. I step back until my backpack rides up against Dylan behind me.

"We're gonna make your life a living, fucking hell, freak."

I close my eyes. I see them both lifting off the floor. Their skulls bash into the ceiling. They drop hard to the ground. Their legs buckle beneath their weight. None of that happens. I don't want it to.

My head cools as Eric steps back.

"We're gonna make you wish you were fucking dead," he says. "And we're gonna enjoy it."

"Yeah," Dylan says, "this is gonna be fun."

Eric stops his retreat. He puts out both his hands. "What? You gonna hit me with your books too? C'mon." He flinches forward to see if I'll flinch back. "I'll fucking feed them to you."

He steps away again.

Dylan circles around to pass him in the hallway.

"We're gonna laugh while you bleed," Eric says, "and everyone else will thank us."

He turns around and follows Dylan quickly down the hall. They turn the corner to the side exit. Their heavy footsteps echo through the narrow passage. Even when I can't see them, I know exactly where they are.

Living hell. Freak. They have no idea.

5

"So, Greg started hopping up and down the stairs, making monkey noises and moving around like," Andre makes big ape-like arm swings. His right hand drops low enough to almost knock over his water glass.

"Honey, be careful at the table," Aida cautions.

"And I got up and yelled at him like, 'C'mon monkey! Get back in the cage!' and followed him around like I had a whip." He throws his arm out to simulate cracking a whip.

"Honey," Aida says again.

Andre tries not to laugh through his story. "I chased him around a few times until he jumped to hide behind Jordan. I pretended like he disappeared and started looking around for him. Then he jumped out like," Andre drops his jaw wide and waves his hands in front of him, "and I'm like," he makes his eyes and mouth big in surprise, "and everyone starts laughing again."

Ben and Aida both sit and listen, Ben chewing casually, Aida keeping a close watch on the plate, glass, and silverware in front of Andre. I take another forkful of beef stir-fry.

"It got so loud that we didn't hear Mr. Reynolds open his door and step outside."

Ben raises an eyebrow. Aida narrows her mouth in anticipation of another maternal lecture. I continue eating.

"Suddenly, everyone went totally quiet and that's when I turned around to see Mr. Reynolds standing there right behind me. I thought I was in so much trouble, but Mr. Reynolds just looked at everyone, nodded at me and said 'Let's get the monkey!' I ran around behind Greg and Mr. Reynolds ran around the other side like, 'Yah! yah!'"Andre makes more whipping motions. He's trying hard to keep it together. "Greg was trying to jump around everyone, but me and Mr. Reynolds were right next to him."

I feel my phone shake in my pocket. Text message. The third I've gotten since dinner started. Might be Evelyn, she's the only one who ever texts. I really, really wanna look but Aida doesn't allow phones at the table. Even Ben can't use his.

"And then Mr. Reynolds points at his door like, 'Go monkey! In the cage!' and Greg starts jumping over there and when he goes inside, Mr. Reynolds closes him in." Andre smiles, looking for someone to enjoy this as much as he is.

Another vibration. Has to be Evelyn. She usually sends short messages very quickly.

"He looked at everyone and went, 'That was really close. He almost escaped.' It was really funny. He stood with his back on the door so Greg couldn't get out." His words stumble.

Aida appears relieved as she goes back to her food.

"Then," Andre's almost shaking now, "Greg knocked on the door and said, 'Okay, let me out.' But Mr. Reynolds said, 'Do you hear something?' Greg's like, 'I wanna come out now.' and Mr. Reynolds pretended that he didn't hear anything for like five minutes before he finally opened the door. Then he was all, 'Oh, hi, Greg, I had nooooo idea you were in there.'" Finally Andre gets to enjoy his laugh.

Ben chuckles, nodding. He glances over at Aida, who smiles, equal parts amusement and relief. It's easily the best dinner we've had in a month. I'm not about to ruin it by mentioning Choi or Eric and Dylan. Those are my secrets. They can have theirs and I'll have mine. It's better that way.

Andre looks around to me, as though seeking approval for his story. "Funny," I say. "Cool teacher to play along like that."

"Yeah," he says, "most of them are really lame and don't let us do anything."

"Totally lame," I say. I scrunch my face at Andre in disgust over just how lame those teachers are. He laughs. Poor kid probably doesn't know a damn thing. It's a shame that he's been caught in the middle of this mess. I wonder if he's aware of who his parents really are.

"I saw a monkey in the wild once," Ben says. He pauses, looking around the table to check that he has our attention. "I was in Cambodia for some training exercises and we decided to take a *tuk-tuk*," he looks at Andre, "the little cabs they have there with a motorcycle that pulls the covered seats. We got out to get some food along the road and when we got back there was a monkey on our seat going through our bags."

"Where was the driver?" Aida asks.

"He was sitting on the curb smoking, watching the monkey go through our stuff."

"What'd you do?" Andre asks.

"I wanted to shoo it away but another guy, I don't remember his name now, said it might get scared and attack."

"Cornered animal," I say quietly.

"How big was it?" Andre asks.

"Oh, maybe two feet tall. But they can be really vicious. They can rip your face off." Ben makes his hand resemble a claw and scratches the air.

"Cool," says Andre.

Ben looks at Aida across from him. She rolls her eyes. He snarls his lips back and makes the scratching motion back at her.

"They can," Ben insists.

"I know," she says. "Too bad they didn't do that to you."

Ben's face and hand both drop at the same time. "That was mean," he says with a pathetic whine.

"Yeah," Aida replies, "but I won't rip your face off."

"True."

"At least not in front of the boys."

I chuckle slightly while lifting another bite. I don't care if the story is true or not. It doesn't matter. Whoever they are, Aida and Ben, Mom and Dad, they could be worse. Brent's parents locked his brother out of the house for a week after they caught him smoking pot in his room. David's stepmom can't wait for him to move out in a couple years—she actually tells him this almost every week—and doesn't care where he goes, so long as he goes. All things considered, the life I have here—the illusion of life I have here—is pretty good. There's another vibration in my pocket.

The first message reads: *everyone hates u.* The sender is odin.lewis.is.a.freak@gmail.com. The next is: *u need to die* from odinshoulddie@gmail.com. *Kill urself or i will.* That one's more funny than threatening. *Its ur fault no 1 likes u freak*, and *make everyone happy and die* come from K1llOdin_23.

It's pretty clear what they're trying to do. It's almost amusing in its desperation. I suppose "KillOdin" could have been taken but is "K1llOdin" so popular that they need a number behind it?

The last message, sent just after I finished cleaning the table and going to my room to study, is a link to a Facebook group called "Odin Lewis is a freak and should die." The members, eight of them, probably more of the "K1llOdin" accounts, have the same picture: last year's yearbook photo with a Photoshopped nine-millimeter pistol pointing at my head. It would be frightening if it weren't so pathetic.

I don't need to look into the past to know exactly who at least two of those members are. Eric and Dylan, probably a couple others from their little group of shitheads. They got my number from David, who hasn't spoken to me since his big humiliation in the lunch room, which also stemmed from pictures on Facebook. Maybe this group is his attempt at poetic justice. He probably thinks the text messages themselves will get me into trouble with my parents. What the idiot doesn't understand is that if I were to get in trouble over messaging, the first thing my parents would do is check the messages being sent, and that's when he'd get caught. I'm glad that won't happen though; the last thing I need is more attention.

Of course, if I'm wrong, if perhaps Eric and Dylan aren't savvy enough to manage a computer and had to ask someone else to work on this for them, it would be a bit harder to track. Past images come to my mind in a flash and I can feel my way to what I'm looking for quickly, but I still need a starting point in my search. Something familiar and certain.

At first I thought I only needed to be able to picture the person's face in order to trace through their history, but it doesn't work that way. I mean, it's not like I can obtain Samuel L. Jackson's bank account information just by watching *The Avengers* again. It might be a proximity thing, like I need to be close to the person, but then I wouldn't be able to follow Eric or Dylan when they're not around, which I can.

It was them. They asked David for my phone number today, told him they wanted to talk to me, then went over to Eric's house right after school to set up a bunch of fake email accounts. Clearly, I must be important to them if they'd spend their entire afternoon plotting ways to make me feel bad. And they think *I'm* a freak. They even got Kevin's other friends, T.J. and Ross, to join in. Not David though. At least he hasn't gone that far. Dylan left after a couple of hours of brainstorming. They're miles away from each other now, at home, in their rooms, talking on the phone. Both of them are a few miles away from me too. Obviously it isn't a proximity thing. Maybe it's familiarity.

I have no idea whether Randall Choi is in town or has flown somewhere else. I picture him, the squarish face and black hair, the narrow nose, freckles on his upper cheeks, and the off-color earpiece.

His voice is clear in my head, the earnest tone of it, the even rhythm and straight-ahead delivery. Everything I know of him is completely clear, even the distant memories of his third grade class and the meetings I wasn't present for. I have them recorded. The rest of it, everything that hasn't been seen, is gone. Feels like I'm being pushed back when I try to see it now. It's like the crash. The image is there but I can't get to it. Makes me wish I'd taken better advantage of having him in the room in front of me. I can't verify his story now even if I tried. I wonder if he knew that. Wendell made it sound so easy, too, like I could do that anytime. Or like he could.

What isn't obvious without looking is whether or not Kevin's involved with sending the messages to my phone and the Facebook group. The most recent post is a Photoshopped picture of the bowling team photo with word balloons pointing from everyone else. *I hate Odin, Odin is such a loser,*

Bowling is for pussies, Odin has no balls, and other such clever little blurbs.

It's quite easy to picture Kevin, easier than Dylan or Eric. I can see the three of them talking on the grass outside of the school one day in sophomore year. Eric watched as I walk along the path into the building. I stopped when my name was called. Evelyn walked up behind me. She wore that plaid skirt a lot that year, until she grew two inches and it got too short. We walked together. Eric got Kevin's attention and pointed with his chin in my direction. Eric said they should kick my ass. I'm weird and a nerd and they'd be doing the whole school a favor if they made me leave forever. Dylan agreed. "Nah," Kevin said, "No way she's interested in that loser." Eric said they should kick my ass anyway. "I like having him around here," Kevin said. "Gives me something to look forward to." Eric nodded and said he understands. He said they'll let Kevin have me then. He'll be like my—he took a moment to think of just the right term—designated ass-kicker.

They all laughed. Eric then said that if Kevin gets me then Eric gets Shawn, one of the overachievers. They laughed again. I was wondering what Eric meant when he said Kevin told them I was his. He didn't remember it correctly. Almost a month later they saw me reading on the basketball court.

Their history is easy to see, but the images don't have the same sharpness as it did when Wendell was in my head. The images are somewhat . . . unfocused.

Mean texts and Facebook groups aren't Kevin's style. He's always more open with his dislike. I mean, he's had my email for years, from when we were kids, but never used it since we stopped being friends. Eric and Dylan didn't even talk to him today. Haven't for the last week in fact. They'd joked about setting up this group for a couple of weeks, but only started today. Guess Kevin's not my designated ass-kicker anymore.

It would be easy enough to stop them. Launch a trash can this time. Drop a table on them. Hell,

I could probably pick up Dylan and use him to hit Eric. If people weren't scared of me already they sure as hell would be after that. Plus, it would attract a lot of attention, probably enough to bring Choi back and then what? Black vans and helicopters? SWAT teams and attack dogs? That would be a pretty badass way to disappear forever. A stupid one, too.

Most people would go to the vice principal with this kind of stuff, but it's not like Faria would want to help. He'd be more inclined to help *them*. I bet I could have a dozen guys kicking the shit out of me in front of Faria and he would give them tips on more efficient beatings, from experience and all.

No, they're right. No one likes me. Not anymore. Not even my friends, Brent, Richard. Not Evelyn. Fuck, I probably ruined any chance with her. Not my classmates, my teachers, my teammates. I doubt my parents trust me anymore. They're all just people I have to be around. I doubt any of them would care if I disappeared, if they weren't required by either law or their superiors to keep their eyes on me. Even Wendell's stopped talking. Pathetic as this little We Hate Odin support group is, they're right.

I shouldn't have fought back. I should've ignored Kevin like usual. Everyone knows that he's full of shit anyway. That's why his rumors about Evelyn didn't stick. I should have blanked them all out and moved on. It's not like they were actually important. Not until I let them become important. Instead, Wendell got into my head so much that I couldn't stop myself.

Fuck. They're right about one other thing too, it is my fault no one likes me.

6

THE FACEBOOK GROUP WAS SHUT DOWN SOMETIME before I woke up yesterday morning, after less than two days online. It had more than twenty members with made-up names and photos that were a variation on a theme: my yearbook photo with a noose around the neck, my face plastered over a wanted poster of Osama bin Laden with "or alive" scratched out, the bowling team with brighter, happier colors and me removed, and me sitting in front of a classroom, as I am now, with crosshairs drawn over. The last one was disturbing as the clothes were those I'd worn that morning. They were creative, I had to give them that.

The messages continued, rarely during school and never during class, which made the culprits pretty fucking obvious, but as soon as classes were over, it was right back to it. The emails are easy to remove without seeing, the texts less so. A few addresses were added, seven in total. Eric, Dylan, and whoever else move randomly between the different accounts. They've started repeating the messages though, both K1llOdin_23 and Die_Odin_Die_16 sent *everyone hates u loser* back-to-back within five minutes of each other last night. The amount of effort going into this routine is amazing. I've done group assignments for classes that didn't work as well together.

I thought about leaving the phone in my room during the day, but reconsidered since there might be an emergency or something. That's what the phone was originally for anyway, even if there's only been one emergency in the three years I've had it. It was the time Ben's mom, Maw Maw, had a stroke and Dad needed to pick me up on the way to the hospital. She still doesn't have complete use of her right arm. Other than that the phone has never lived up to its purpose. Still, better to have it with me. Leaving it in the house, even in my room, could lead to Aida finding it, checking the messages I keep getting, and then a lot of questions that none of us want to answer. Instead, I silenced the ring for text messages and keep it with me. Funny that a month ago I knew exactly who any message was from and looked forward to them. Now I still know exactly who they're from, and try not to look.

Wendell's been quiet too. Can't say I miss him but, well, it does amplify the silence. You know you're completely alone when even the voice in your head gives you the silent treatment.

I shift a bit to let the pressure off my elbows, resting my forearms on my knees instead. It's interesting how you can guess who's passing by their ankles and the type of shoes they wear. Brand-new Nike high tops, black boots with straps across the front, open-toed sandals with butterflies on them, my own beat-up canvas skate shoes, even though I've skated maybe twice in my entire life and not well. I always wondered why people would put so much effort into what goes on their feet, such a small and distant part of the body, but now I know. It's to grab the attention of people with nothing better to do but stare at the ground. It's to appeal to the introverts and outcasts. To make the wearers feel like they're better than us because we're staring at the ground and they're not. Then, a pair of polished black wingtips appear.

"Good morning, Odin," says the voice above me. I look up to see Principal Hauser. He's not a particularly menacing figuring, not like Faria. He's got a pot belly, a thick gray beard, thin gray hair, and remarkably blue eyes. It's the first thing most people notice about him, when they're not staring at the ground. "How are you this morning?"

"Fine," I say, arching back so I can see him.

"Have you heard anything from that M.I.T. recruiter yet?"

The images come to me, but still aren't as clear as before.

Four years ago, when Daryl Corker killed himself, Hauser spent the better part of two months crying and drinking. His wife tried to comfort him at first but decided it was better to leave him alone in his study with his old books and dusty records of Glenn Miller and Art Tatum, which he didn't listen to because they were too upbeat. He started a journal, writing by hand in a hard leather notebook. He wrote about his time as a teacher, vice principal, and principal. He wrote about how he'd hoped that Corker would be his successor but instead the position went to "this pushy, overbearing upstart who too often thinks a teenager is the same thing as a criminal." The drinking, crying, writing, these were his way of getting out every bit of sadness, every little bit of frustration and annoyance that he'd been bottling up for years, decades, in one mass catharsis. They were his Wendell. At Corker's funeral he called him "a friend, an inspiration, but more than anything, a teacher who dedicated his entire life to the betterment of our community of Man." After that, he took a week to dry out, both his face and his liver, tore apart every page from the journal, and returned to school with a smile.

"Nothing yet," I say.

Really. The moment his foot hit the teacher parking lot pavement outside of his 2005 Buick, he looked at the building and smiled. He's been trying to do the same every morning ever since. Trying.

"It was only a few days ago," he says, "I'm sure they'll be in touch."

I nod.

"I'm surprised they would come all the way out here so early in the application process." He furrows his brow. "They must really want you in their program."

"They must," I say.

He looks up at the ceiling, then at the wall over my head. "Would be a shame to waste such an opportunity now."

He's talking like he knows something about the "M.I.T. recruiter," but I know he doesn't.

"Hmmm?" he says, looking down at me again.

"I guess so."

"Better start trying then. You can't slack just because you're almost done here." He smiles with one side of his face. "Not until at least the last half of senior year. Right?"

" . . . I'm not sure how to answer that," I hazard.

He nods. "You're a smart one."

He looks around to the other students starting to file into their classes and those still at their lockers changing their books and checking their hair or make-up. "Well," he says down to me, "I'd better get going. And so should you."

He starts away, hands held together behind him as he walks. It's then that I finally notice the way his feet sound different than everyone else's. While other steps are rushed stomps, his are light, almost lilting, double taps against the tile. He knows exactly where he's going and he's in no hurry to get there.

Everyone else is in a hurry as soon as classes are done. After so many years, I barely notice how the foot stomps, slamming lockers, and shouted chatter echo through the hallway to an almost deafening extent. Even in class, when the teacher's trying to eke out an extra couple of minutes, the noise is overwhelming and everyone, except for the suck-ups which every class has, itches to join in. Not me. I take my time packing my bag, looking at the old posters on the wall—I never went to any of the school dances or bake sales, probably should have—and walking to my locker. By the time I've entered the combination, the noise has begun to die. It's quiet enough to hear the rushed steps toward me. I look over quickly and I flinch as Brent pounds out one last stomp and then stops immediately before reaching me.

"Yo," he says, standing with his head titled back slightly. This position makes the difference in his nostrils clear.

"Hey," I say as uninterested as possible.

"How ya been?"

I look around at the blur of motion which I'm not a part of.

"Fine, I guess."

"I heard you've been holding your own little rebellion in classes. Sounds crazy."

He looks at me like he actually cares.

"You know what," I say, "you don't have to do this."

"Do what?"

"Act like you give a fuck."

"Dude, I'm sorry, okay? I just didn't know how to react."

The noise decreases as more students move down the hall toward the door.

"I mean, you went from being, like, the quiet, smart guy to sending another kid to the hospital with, like, a fractured skull or something."

I mutter, "It wasn't a fractured skull."

"I'm not saying Kevin didn't deserve that but, you know, it's pretty scary. It's, like, no one knew you could do that."

"Yeah," I say, "I didn't either."

"Then you're like yelling at teachers and shit. Don't get me wrong, it's pretty funny some of the things you said. Did you really correct Mr. Steiner's use of Macavelian?"

"Machiavellian," I say.

He shakes his head. "Dude, that's the kinda stuff I think everyone wishes they could do." He looks around almost wistfully. "But it's totally unlike anything we'd seen you do before. We didn't know if something was up or how to deal with it. Figured we'd give you some space to go back to normal on your own or something."

Normal. That's not even an option.

I could look into everything he's saying. His past might not be as sharp in my mind as it could be, but it would still show if I should trust him. It's not like Brent hasn't lied to me before. Days when he said he was sick when really he was busy gaming with other friends, or how he never mentioned the crush he had on Evelyn in freshman year; lies, but harmless ones. I probably should check his latest excuse, but I don't. That would be betraying him. Even if we haven't talked since his previous lame excuse for not coming to my birthday party, that doesn't mean we're enemies. Not like Kevin and I, or Kevin, Eric, Dylan, and, apparently, David and I. They're friends, David and Brent, but they haven't been too close for a while. No, I need to be better than that. He's still a friend after all.

"Wait," I say, "who's we?"

"Everyone, you know? Richard, Mike, Teddy, Terri, Lucas, all of them. Evelyn's been asking around about you too, trying to see if you're okay."

"What about David?"

"He hasn't been talking much. The thing about his cousin and all, Teddy and them were really riding him for that. He took it pretty hard. He's not even online very often these days, or maybe like changed his gamertag or something."

"Shit. Sorry about that."

"Whatever, he should get over it."

I nod. Didn't think my retaliation to David's teasing would have that kind of effect. It was something to get attention away from me. Like with Faria, or with Kevin. Didn't expect it to get that far.

"You cool to hang for a bit?" Brent asks.

"Yeah, I'm all right."

"Cool," he says. He looks around the hall, at the few students taking their time to exit the building, and the couple acting like no one can see them making out behind the open locker. "Let's maybe go somewhere else," he says, watching the two of them trying to swallow the other's tongue.

"Let's do that," I say.

We wander toward the administrative wing at the back of the building. We move slowly, nothing better to do.

"So," he says after a minute, "don't you want to know what Evelyn's been saying?"

I sigh. "Probably not."

"Nah man, not like that. She's been worried. She cares. That's good."

"Yeah?"

"Yeah. After your party and stuff she was asking if you hated her for not going like she promised."

"I don't hate her."

"That's what I said. How many people came to the party anyway?"

"Not many."

"Sorry."

"I'm over it."

"But yeah, she's been asking if you're okay."

"She could just ask me herself."

He stops walking and waits for me face him. "You smashed a kid's face in with a backpack." He looks scared as he speaks. "He left a trail of blood that one of the janitors had to clean with a mop. That's not something people forget."

I feel myself deflate. "Yeah," I sigh.

"It's hard not to remember what happened every time we pass the benches or mention you to anyone."

"I understand," I say, regretfully.

He kicks into motion. "She said it was actually pretty cool how you stood up to Kevin like that, though. Before it got scary."

He stops at the intersection where the central hall splits to the lunch room on the right and the exit to the basketball court and auditorium on the left, the stairs on either side of us before the hall leading to the health room and the administration offices. He looks around. The janitor with the long hair is sweeping the floor down the hall. The lunch room is already locked, classes upstairs will be locked soon, too, except those used by clubs. He gestures toward to the side exit with the covered window that makes it impossible to see anything but a shadow directly behind it. I shrug. He leads on.

"Yeah, other than that it's just the same old shit."

I nod.

He stops again. "So, what *has* been happening with you?"

"Nothing," I say. "Family stuff."

"Yeah?"

"Yeah."

"Like what?"

"I can't really talk it about."

"Not even a little bit?" he asks.

"I shouldn't. It doesn't affect you anyway. It's just me."

"That's not true," he mutters.

"What?"

"I mean, when you're like angry and stuff, we all

feel it. And then combined with seeing what you did to Kevin. We all get scared. It's like knowing there's someone around you carrying a gun. At any moment they could just decide to kill you, and you can't stop them."

"I didn't mean that."

"I know," he says. "You just don't know what it's like." He starts toward the exit again. We're not supposed to use this door to get from one building to the other but everyone does. It saves time. It's locked on the outside and automatically closes, so people coming into the building have to walk all the way around to the front or get someone to open it from the inside. It's an attempt to prevent truancy.

"It's not like I'm dangerous or anything," I say. "I'm not a monster."

He stops again. "That's just it though, we don't know that. You just suddenly changed in this completely unimaginable way. Like a totally different person."

"It's not like I would hurt any of you guys."

"That's good to know," he says as he starts walking again.

"I don't want to hurt anyone. Not really."

"Promise?" he says, as we walk past the last classroom before the exit.

"Yeah. Especially not you or Evelyn."

"Cool." He motions with his head for us to go outside. He drops slightly behind. We take the next several steps in silence. I reach out to push the exit open.

"Please, remember you said that," he says.

I nod as my hand hits against the pressure bar of the door.

"And I'm sorry," he says. "They made me do it."

Brent shoves me hard into the door. The handle bangs and rattles as the door opens. The sun coats everything in a stunning light.

"I'm so sorry!" I hear. "They forced me!" The door slams shut.

I see the shapes before the light fades. Eric in front of me, Dylan and Ross on one side, T.J. on the other, then David. An elbow pins me against the door.

"See?" Eric growls into my face. "Even your best friend doesn't like you."

It's like my throat's about to pop. Eric's forearm, his full weight behind it, presses against my larynx. My back arches over the bag pressed against the wall behind me. I feel the air pushing out. The only breaths are his, on my face.

I struggle to speak. "No. Please, don't."

"We're going to fucking kill you," he whispers.

"You don't," I gasp, "know." Nothing. There's nothing around me.

His mouth moves but there's no sound. I hear my pulse against his arm. It throbs through my head. My weight starts to fall forward. My lower back strains from leaving the stretch. I hear a noise. See a blur.

"—Can't fucking breathe!"

The pressure lightens. I swallow air.

"That's the point, dumbass," Eric says.

"Yeah, dumbass," says Dylan.

"He's not going anywhere," says someone else, Ross I think. "Just get this shit over with."

The arm is still across my collar, but the force of the push is less intense. Enough to breathe at least, see my surroundings, the mad faces, the hate in Eric's eyes in front of me. He's so close I can feel the wind when he blinks.

"Little fucking freak deserves this," he says.

"You're not killing anyone," Ross replies. "That's stupid."

"You on his side now?" Eric yells.

"Nah, I'm just saying."

***

I can't help seeing it, as a blur. Lunch today. David pulled Brent aside. "Take Odin down the side exit fifteen minutes after school today."

"Why?" Brent asked.

"Because we have business with him."

"Fuck you," said Brent.

"Why do you care?" asked David. "You're not even friends anymore. He's a fucking freak. He doesn't belong here." Brent shook his head. "Look," David said, "someone is going home bloody today. If it isn't him, it's gonna be you."

"Why?" Brent asked.

"For being on his side. So it's your choice. Is freak boy worth the pounding?"

Brent thought for a moment.

"Side exit?" Brent asked. "Fifteen minutes after school?"

"Yeah." Brent hung his head as David walked away.

"Who fucking cares what happens to him?" Eric yells.

"No one," Dylan says, "no one fucking cares."

I see David at the corner of my eyes. He stares

coldly. There are miles between us. He sees me looking and glances toward the others.

"We're going to beat you so badly, your parents won't recognize you." Eric says. He presses his forehead against mine. His arm crushes my neck.

"You shouldn't," is all I can think to say.

He laughs. He looks at one of the others over his shoulder. Probably Dylan.

"Don't know what you're doing," I say. They probably hear it differently: Don't. No. What're you doing?

He turns back. "Tell you what, every good reason you give me not to pound you into pulp is one tooth I'll leave in your empty fucking head."

A dozen immediately come to mind, but only one they'd understand. "Kevin," I say.

I see his eye twitch.

"What I did."

His teeth, like a wolf.

"I can do worse."

"Yeah," he says. He thumps his head against mine. "Try it."

No choice. "I'll break your arm." I growl at him. "Break it in half."

Eric laughs again.

I look at the others. "Every one of you. I'll throw you into the street." I hope this works without Wendell in my mind. It'll be tragic if my abilities sputter now.

I peek over at David. He's still looking away. "You," I say, "you first." Back to Eric. "You last."

"You heard him," Eric says, leaning away and glancing to David. "You first."

I don't see the hit but I feel it. Hard. Against my cheek. Wrenching my neck. My head bounces off the door. A second punch lands on my nose. A crush then the feeling that I have to sneeze. A kick buckles my knee. My backpack pulls me sideways. I collapse to the ground. My thigh smacks the concrete and I feel it up my whole leg. My head snaps back again. I know I'm bleeding. I can hear the air moving before the fist comes. I can hear the air.

I can make them stop.

I see the next fist in flight, David's. I picture a wall between us. The punch stops. His hand pushes back. They all stop. They take one step away.

"You first," I say again.

I picture his hand twisting completely over at the wrist. He screams as the bones snap. His head slams against the wall.

"The fuck?" someone says. Probably Ross.

I throw David onto the ground. He moans.

Ross takes another step away. T.J. too. Eric looks around at them. Dylan looks at him. Dylan. I flip his feet out from under him. He collapses like a ragdoll.

"Nah, man, nah," says Ross.

I move a finger to spin Dylan's foot until his ankle pops.

Ross runs. T.J. starts away as well. I throw an

arm out and see him snap forward like a force blast hitting his torso from behind.

Eric twitches back and forth. His eyes huge with panic and disbelief.

"You last."

I squeeze my fist. I hear every bone in his hand crack.

The door bumps me from behind. Someone yells my name.

I flick my wrist up. Eric screams as his as forearm bends in half.

Men in black gear rush in behind him. Several men surround all of us just outside the building. They pull Eric and the others away. The men wear helmets with visors that cover their faces. There's motion everywhere. A flurry of bodies and arms and legs and hands holding guns. One of the men yells, "Down, down, down!" I don't have time to move.

The door bumps me from behind so hard that I start to fall forward. Hands wrap under my arms to pull me backward through the doorway. "Take him," I hear from behind. One arm crosses my chest and another pulls the bag strap, yanking me back. I twist to see nothing but thick sleeves and the school walls around me. The men in black keep the boys pinned to the grass outside. David groans. Dylan shouts, holding his ankle. Eric screams. Half his arm dangles freely. One of the men rushes forward. I see myself in the plastic over his face. Bewildered. I also see the men behind me, two of them. They each have one hand around my chest pulling me back and another hand pointing a long gun in the air. The man in front of me outside nods once before slamming the door shut.

I'm on the floor now. My legs extend to just inside the school's side exit. The paper covering the window keeps everything but the light from coming in. I'm left sitting on the ground, staring at the dim afternoon sun through the paper. There are shoe scuffs on the bottom of the door.

I hear a harsh breath from behind. I want to turn but I don't. I know who it is and I know what he wants. I don't need to confirm my suspicions. Not yet. Let me have this moment of peace for a long as possible.

"Leave us." I hear behind me.

"Sir?"

"Go."

I brace myself to stand. I turn at last to see two of the men in black combat gear moving toward the main hall. And there's Randall Choi. I straighten my back and then raise my head to see him.

"You okay?" he asks.

Black suit and everything. Cell phone in his hand. Nothing else I can see.

"Hey, Odin," he says. "You okay?"

"Ye—" I start. "Yeah."

"Good. Follow me."

He turns and begins down the narrow passage.

The men in the black gear are gone. Their footsteps are barely audible in the hall.

The dim light through the covered window falls in a stretched square on the floor. Trapezoid. A dull

124

yellow on the off-white linoleum, dark lines of the scuffs and scratches permanently etched into the surface. My shadow cuts through the light shaft. I'm long and thin and missing my head.

"Hey!" Choi stands there, arms hanging easy at his sides. "Follow me."

7

I WIPE AT THE SHARP PAIN IN MY CHEEK. MY HAND pulls away bloody. I wipe again and my hand is mostly clean. The pain still throbs in the spot where David landed the first shot. I check my nose next. It doesn't feel cracked or broken. It's more itchy on the inside than anything. Hard to tell where the blood is coming from. Doesn't look like the cut is too bad. Not like before. Not like Kevin. Then there's the pain in my knee and ribs, from the kicks. Present but minor compared to the side of my face. More than anything, the blows to the ribs and knee make my backpack feel heavier. No stains on my clothes. Must not be too bad.

Choi pushes open the one of the double doors to the lunch room. Those doors were supposed to have been locked fifteen minutes before classes ended.

"How're you doing?" he asks. He's only a few inches taller than I am. I hadn't noticed that before.

I give my best "the fuck you think?" look.

"Hurt much?" He gestures vaguely around the level of my face.

"A little bit," I say sarcastically, wiping at my cheek and glancing at the fresh blood on my hand.

"We'll get that taken care of in a couple minutes," he says as he gives the door a shove and steps away. I use my elbow to stop it from closing on me. I'm sure the janitorial staff will appreciate not having to wipe my blood off the door. Meanwhile, Choi couldn't even hold the door open for the injured.

"Make sure that closes," he says, walking toward the empty tables.

I watch as the one door shuts into the other. "Close the door behind you" seems to be the theme of the last few days.

"You want anything?" Choi continues moving to the other side of the room. "From the vending machine," he says. "A drink or a snack?"

"Nothing."

"I'll get you something. Sit down."

It's weird being here with no other students. I can visualize each group in their chosen spot, or the place they were the last time I spent lunch in here, back when I sat with Brent and David, the traitors, and Richard; I have no idea what happened with him.

I shuffle to the table closest to the door where the Honor Roll girls usually sit. It's one away from Evelyn and the theatre girls. Picturing them there, her and everyone else, all the way to the football players in the back, it's a completely different angle than I'm used to, being stuck at my table as I am. Or was. I let my bag drop to the floor.

Choi's voice echoes from the other side of the large hall. "I'm happy students have healthier snacks but can't there be at least one machine that sells soda?" He's chattier than I'd expect. Still just as measured, but almost friendly.

"Whatever," I mutter.

From here, I'd see nothing but Evelyn's back, her long hair hanging down, maybe the shapes of her shoulders, waist and hips. They're nice but that's not what makes her interesting. It's like empty space. Just color and form with little else occupying it. None of the character and life that really pulls me in. Like the room itself. Empty. It's strange, I've seen this room almost every day for three years, yet it's unfamiliar from here. Big and blank and quiet. Tables with nothing to hide their piss-yellow tops. Lifeless. The exact opposite of normal.

The big windows in the back of the cafeteria provide a view of the teacher parking lot, the street that connects to the loop around the side of the campus, and the houses across that street. Trees sway lightly in the wind, but otherwise nothing moves. There are a few cars still in the lot. Must be office staff and teachers whose clubs meet at this time. Evelyn's friend Lori is in the Photography Club which should have a meeting today. Pretty sure they aren't talking about shutters and lenses right now.

Choi's footsteps approach. "Here," he says, holding out a handful of napkins. "For your eye."

"My eye?"

"Yeah," he says, standing on the opposite side of the bench and pushing the napkins toward me again. "It's bleeding."

"I thought it was my cheek."

"It's just under the eye. Doesn't look too bad."

I take the napkins and press them against half my face, from the top of the eyebrow to the bottom of the cheekbone. I still feel a throb from the impact. My nose isn't so itchy anymore.

"I also got you this." Choi places a plastic bottle of apple juice on the table. "Don't know if you like it but thought it would be nice to have something."

"I thought you knew everything about me," I say.

"No one does, Odin. No one does."

He looks around the room. He still has his ear-piece. I point in its general direction.

"Is it for the phone?"

He shakes his head. "It's so I can hear." He cocks his head. "You didn't know that?"

"Should I have?"

"Hmm," he says.

He didn't have trouble speaking, he had trouble hearing. He's right, I should have figured that out. Doesn't explain anything about his position now, but you never know. Chain of events and all. If his classmates hadn't made fun of him, maybe he would have never started at speech clubs, and maybe he wouldn't be here now.

I pull the napkins back to check the damage. A slightly curved line of blood falls unevenly into the grain of the napkin, forming a crude smile.

"Look," Choi says to grab my attention. "We'll have a medic here in a while but first, we need to talk and I need to apologize."

While I'm slumped forward with my head in my hand, napkin back over my face, he's sitting straighter than any student I've seen on these benches.

"We devoted most of our effort to making sure that you wouldn't harm others nearby but didn't consider what they might do to you. We knew that there would be danger if people knew of your abilities, but assumed they'd be outside of the environment. This situation is a bit more . . . barbaric . . . ordinary, than we anticipated."

"Isn't that exactly what you wanted for me? Ordinary?"

"That's not an option. Not after today."

I look to the back to the empty room. I'll probably never see it this way again.

"I tried to tell them."

"It's not your fault, Odin. We know you tried. It's everyone else who wasn't willing to let you remain unnoticed. We always wanted to be as unobtrusive as possible for this exact reason, but the situation with those boys out there, we had no choice."

"I know," I say, even though I don't.

I don't know what I would have done if those men hadn't stopped me. First there was David, his wrist snapping, his head bouncing off the side of the building. The bones in Dylan's ankle are definitely broken. I let Ross go but not T.J. I wanted to get him. I didn't even think about how much force to hit him with, I just wanted to hit him. Then Eric. I crushed his fingers like an aluminum can. His bones popped like firecrackers. His arm broke clean in half. I still see it. Only skin keeping the forearm together.

"Are they all right?" I ask, feeling the ache of each blow.

"You have to ask?" he says.

I don't. The men, a dozen of them, wear the black uniforms of federal police. Flak jackets with a pair of pockets along the front, visors to protect their faces, and two belts, one extending down the thigh to a sidearm. Pistols on their legs and rifles in their hands. Loaded with tranquilizers and stun darts. Guns all the same. It was so much more than I could have imagined. A schoolyard fight is one thing, but one with armored officers with tear gas grenades is completely different. I never thought anything I did could escalate like that.

They're being treated right now, or at least they were within the last second, the most recent time I can see. Except for Ross. He was tackled and is now sitting in the field outside the door being questioned by a pair of officers. David isn't bleeding at least, just a nasty bump. He's already got his wrist braced and bandaged. Another agent is getting his personal information to contact his parents. The medic, a woman wearing a uniform without the headgear and vest, twists Dylan's ankle and asks if it hurts. The response is a quick cry of pain. The medic turns it a different way and asks again. "Goddammit, yes! It all hurts!"

Eric isn't there. He's in an emergency vehicle, a black one, like an SUV, something less likely to attract attention than an ambulance. He got a shot of morphine to numb the pain. They tell him it'll only take a few minutes and then he won't feel anything. He'll get some x-rays and possibly need a couple of metal rods put in his arm. It shouldn't be a problem, the agent says, he'll just have to mention the rods before boarding a plane. Eric lies on the stretcher with a sleepy smile on his face.

"They'll be fine," says Choi. "We'll contact their parents and get it all straightened out soon. The others as well." He means the Photography Club, the office staff, the people in the neighboring houses. They were ushered away during the fight.

"What will they say happened?"

"Whatever we want them to," he says flatly.

I close my eyes. I can play the entire scene over and over again in my mind a thousand times simultaneously: the forearm across my throat, the gasping, the threats. Instead all I hear are snapping bones. So quick and easy. Little pops. I imagined the empty space moving David's wrist, Dylan's foot, Eric's arm, and it happened. Snapping fingers like snapping fingers. I could have thrown them into the air, crushed their chests, twisted their necks completely around. I could have killed them without landing one punch.

The napkin catches one tear but not the other. I feel it hanging there at the top of my cheek.

"I didn't," I say without knowing what would follow. "I didn't . . ."

"I know," Choi says. "We know."

I keep my head down so he won't see me crying.

"It's not your fault."

The drop rolls down to my mouth. "I couldn't stop them," I say.

"Hey, we don't blame you. Do you understand?"

I inhale sharply with my nose.

"You tried to restrain yourself as much as

possible. We know that. None of this was your choice." He pauses. I see the shadow of his hand moving closer to me, like he's trying to reach out but doesn't quite make it. "But we also know that nothing like this can ever happen again."

I sniffle. "What does that—"

The door behind me creaks open. I wipe the tear away quickly before turning.

At the door, holding it open, is the long-haired janitor. He still has a rag hanging from his front pocket. The medic, the woman without the helmet and vest, steps around him from behind.

The janitor nods once at Choi. He makes sure the door closes behind him.

"Wiggins?" I ask.

"You could have known if you wanted."

The medic motions for me to turn my back on the table. She's in her early thirties with brown hair in a ponytail and a very kind face. She places her medical kit on the ground and kneels next to it.

"Let me see," she says. She holds her rubber-gloved hands in my view to show she's not a threat.

"How's it look?" Choi asks from over my shoulder.

"Better than the others," she says. She has green eyes that become lighter from the center out. "Maybe about six or seven stitches. Does it hurt?"

"A little bit."

"You don't have to be a tough guy," she says. Her thumb brushes across my cheek, the one with the tears, not the one with the blood. "It hurts?"

"Yeah," I say. "It hurts a lot."

8

AFTER A BIT OF CLEAN UP, IT DOESN'T LOOK TOO bad. Seven stitches hold together a slivered curve tracing the bottom of my left eye socket. The medic joked that when I got older and found a job I won't even be able to notice it with the other lines and bags under my eyes from age and fatigue. It's puffy and red but other than that, nothing awful.

My leg and ribs are bruising where they kicked me. It feels tight when I breathe and it's uncomfortable to twist. At least nothing is broken. Not like them. All things considered, I came out of it pretty well unscathed. Physically at least.

Choi sits on the other side of the benches when I exit the bathroom, the far end of the room from the main door. He leans against the table as he watches me approach. It's the closest I've ever seen him to relaxed. "Feel better now?" he asks.

"Kind of."

"Good." He motions for me to sit across from him, my back to the entrance, as we were after the medic left. He even brought my backpack to the new location with him. I look up at the clock positioned in the center overhang at the front of the student seating area. We've been here for almost forty minutes, most of that time spent putting a needle and string into my face. It stings, but not as bad as the initial hit. I take my seat. He straightens up and slides his phone in his suit pocket.

"So here's what's going to happen," Choi says. "We're going to leave here and take you home. You can pack up whatever you really need, say goodbye to your parents and brother, and then we're—"

"Goodbye?"

"Or something else if you want."

"What are you talking about?"

"Our plans for taking you in."

I furrow my brow at him.

"We can no longer allow you to remain outside like this. Not after today."

I narrow my eyes. "You said it wasn't my fault."

"Fault isn't our concern."

"It should be! If this isn't my fault, then I haven't done anything wrong."

Choi says nothing. He just sits there, straight up and expressionless.

"You told me that if I stopped acting up and didn't attract attention, then you'd leave me alone. So I put aside everything that happened, everything from the day I got here, and went on like nothing was wrong, because of you." I stab one finger toward him. I feel as though the last month's worth of anger and frustration, the mounting fury over every betrayal building to this one, demands release right now. "You told me that if I went along with your arrangement, I'd be allowed to remain here. You said we'd never talk about it again. You told me that, face to face. I can recite the whole fucking conversation word for word!" I fling an arm in the direction of the door behind us. "It's not my fault those assholes wanted to fight me. And there was nothing else I could do to stop them."

He still says nothing.

"So I did everything you asked. Everything!" I pound my first on the table. "I was doing exactly what you told me to! You don't know what those fuckers were saying. I could have done so much more to them. I could have, easily, but I didn't, because you," I emphasize, jabbing the finger back at his face, "told me that if I was quiet and didn't attract attention, then you'd leave me alone!"

"Circumstances have changed."

"Bullshit!" I bang the table again, harder. "You said we had an understanding. I remember it, you made me repeat it over and over."

"I remember that too," he says ever so fucking clearly.

"That was the deal!" I could take him out right now. Do the same thing I did to Kevin, bag to the face and let him bleed. "I did everything you asked!"

"I'm sorry," he says, lying, "but the situation has changed."

I throw my arms out in confusion. "What's changed?"

"You exposed your abilities to at least a dozen civilians—"

"None of them will say anything!" I can't help yelling while he remains unmoved. He has the advantage, and that makes it even worse. "You said that too, that they'll say whatever you tell them. No one here will believe them anyway, so what's the point?"

"The point is we can't risk—"

"The point is that you never wanted to leave me alone! You always wanted to control me!" It's exactly what Wendell was saying. The whole time. It takes all my control to keep from launching this bench at him, smashing it over him, tossing him against the wall and squeezing this bench across his chest until either it breaks or he does. As I should have done in Hauser's office. "That's why you kept watching me all the time! You've always been trying to control me. Everything I do. Everything I think was you and your fucking project making me think that! Like I ever had a fucking choice!"

"That's not true."

"Even this! Even this fucking deal was you controlling me!" I feel the spit flying from my mouth. He's lucky that's all. "I knew it but I let that happen because if I did what you said—you fucking said yourself—then you'd let me go!"

"Look, Odin," he places his hands out to show just how nonthreatening he is. Like he's the Dalai Lama here to enlighten me about my foolishness. "We understand this isn't exactly what we agreed to, but for your own safety—"

"*My* safety?" I say, eyes wide with fake shock. "Right, this all for my safety. Being a prisoner everywhere I go is for my safety. You ever think that maybe I would be safer if you all just went away?"

"You know tha's—" I see him starting to crack.

"No, you can't do that because then I'd be a threat. Well you know what?" My tone goes from mockery to anger. "Good. Maybe you should leave now—"

"Okay, some un get ear," his words jumble.

"—for your own fucking safety."

"Ahmah ne some un nuh—"

There's an echoing boom behind me. The cafeteria doors nearly shatter as they burst open. The black uniforms rush through. Four of them, one in front with three behind. The leader holds his left arm extended sideways as though barring the others. His right arm keeps his pistol angled down.

I freeze seeing them approach. I need to move before they get here. Guaranteed they'll fire if I try to run.

"You're a smart kid," says Choi, "don't do anything dumb."

I look back at him. I feel the snarl on my face. He's regained his composure enough to speak clearly and refrain from moving. "I'm so tired of people saying that," I say.

"No one wants to hurt you. You're too—"

I stand up as they reach the first of the lunch tables, where Choi and I sat earlier. It's lucky he decided to move. He probably didn't expect this to happen. I step over the bench into the space between table. The black uniforms approach on one side, and Choi is seated across the table on the other. I keep my hands out and ready for action on either side.

Choi pushes against the table to stand. He yells across the room, "Priority: Secure the package unharmed!" The agents grow closer. They fan out into two groups of two, splitting as they enter the grid of lunch tables. I position myself between the two duos as best as possible. "Under absolutely no circumstances is lethal force to be used."

"Yes sir," says the lead agent.

"You should just come with us," Choi says. "It would be better for everyone." His words rush but don't jumble. I glance back to see a flurry of motion. Choi lunges over the table behind me, a crackling sound nearby. The electric current of a hand taser forks between round ends. It stops in the air, a wall between us.

I flip the table to push Choi back. No reason to restrain myself anymore. I fling both arms out and the two tables in front of me launch off the ground. Three of the black uniforms go down. The fourth steadies his arm, stun gun in hand. I use the air to push his arm upward. Two wires spring toward the ceiling, electrical current buzzing the entire way. I lift my bag from the seat and launch it at him. Another strike.

I run. Around the remaining table. Out the main doors. They're cracked from where the agents kicked them open. Across the hall is the side exit Brent led me down. I see shadows on the paper covering the window. There's motion at the front, all the way down by the senior benches. More uniforms on the way. I hear footsteps on the stairs between the first and second floors. I dash for the offices at the back of the school.

Ms. O'Hara's usually here for a few hours after classes are over. Faria and Hauser, too. Not today. Files are left on the receptionist's desk. A cup of coffee with lipstick stains. Didn't even have time to close and lock their office doors. Maybe that's what Choi meant about exposure.

I race into Hauser's office and grab one of the chairs as tightly as I can. I sat in this same chair only a few days ago when Choi promised to leave me alone. I hold it up by the legs, feeling the wood grain on my palms and fingers. I take a few steps for momentum and swing at the window. All the frames on the wall drop and shatter on the ground. My ribs strain from the stretch.

"Can I break this?" I mutter to no one.

I take another run and swing. I scream as pain shoots up and down my side. The window shatters. I rattle the chair back and forth to clear some glass from the window frame. I throw the chair down and lunge for the opening.

What's left are the slivers. I press down on the window frame. The glass pierces my hands. I pull myself onto the window. The skin of my palms opens. Head and shoulders through. One leg over. The other leg catches the wall. My bloodied hand slips. It slides across the shattered glass. I tumble forward. I hit the concrete with my shoulder and back. I groan, standing. Stiff and sore. I try not to look at my hands. I shake them instead. Drops of blood spray onto the ground.

"Are you there?" I ask the voice in my head. "Shouldn't you help?"

Behind Hauser's office are metal sheds and exposed pipes, separated from the parking lot by a chain link fence, with several signs facing away from me: *Keep Out, Maintenance Staff Only, No Entry*. A big lock secures the gate. Exposed pipes make the whole area several degrees hotter than anywhere else. I keep my bleeding palms out as I rush to the fence. Maybe six feet high. Three steps and jump. The fence rattles as I grab onto it. One leg over. Careful with the other. Can't fall again. I drop roughly to the ground, take a second to recover, and scramble for the road.

"Where are you?"

Open street ahead. Teacher parking lot with a few cars. Nothing else. The road ahead runs perpendicular to the school. It intersects the curve along the side of campus. A few guards circle outside the auditorium. "Hey!" one yells. I run.

My feet slap the ground. I keep my head down as I move. Wind rushes past my ears. The air stings my hands. Trees and houses blur by. I hear only my breath and footsteps. Where am I going? What am I doing? Have to get away from them but where?

I slow to a jog. The baseball field across the street. Empty. Everything is empty.

"Where do I go?"

Not home, obviously. Not Brent's or Richard's or any other house that I know. Not the bowling alley or movie theater or any usual spots. They'll be there. The ominous *they*. Can't stay here. Houses with closed garages and fences. I take off again. Every step is heavy. If I can make it to the park maybe I can lose them in the trees. If I can't . . .

"Are you there?" I say under my breath. "Help me."

It was stupid to run. Should have stayed and listened. Could have reasoned a way out. Like with Faria. Used what I know, what I can learn, to angle for another deal, a deal Choi would have to follow. Instead I got angry at him. Threatened him. No wonder he called for guards. Stupid. So fucking stupid! Especially for the "smart kid." Shouldn't have run but can't go back now. If they catch me then that's it. They'll take me away. Lock me up somewhere. Make me their prisoner.

Keep moving. Chest burning. Body aching. Been a long time since I've run this much. Barely passed the two-mile test last year. Sprints were always better. Like in football. Not like cross country. Evelyn would be good at this. Evelyn. She'll never look at me the same. If she ever looks at me again.

"If you're real, you'll help me," I mutter as I push ahead.

The thump in my chest makes me afraid to look at my hands. My palms are damp. My fingers are cold.

School far behind. Long road ahead. Nothing but houses with their locked doors, big fences, blue recycling bins, orange and yellow flowers, and satellite television dishes. Different models but the same. Variations on a theme.

There's no traffic. Nothing. Nothing but me and a thumping sound all around. A helicopter above the school. They have a damn helicopter!

Fuck. Fuck! I run. Keep running. If I can get to the park and get under the trees, I can lose them there. Maybe then Wendell will fucking talk to me. Tell me what to do.

Mistake to run. I should stop now. Lay on the ground and give myself up. They could follow the blood trail right to me. Can't stop my hands from bleeding. Can't stop moving. Can't run anywhere.

"Goddammit, Wendell, where are you?" I say between breaths. "Help me!"

Every step stretches my legs and side. Feels like the muscles are going to tear. Thin bands ready to break. I slow to a jog. Then to a walk. I walk because there's nothing else I can do.

"Please," I say. "Please help."

I look around as though he'll suddenly appear floating above me like an angel descending from the sky. I hold my bloody palms out, begging for scraps. "What can I do? Show me where to go." He doesn't answer. Like he never existed at all. Maybe he didn't. Maybe he really was a figment of my imagination the whole time. A construct of a traumatized brain that couldn't heal itself.

"You asshole." I say to Wendell, to myself, to whoever is there. "You started this."

The helicopter moves in a circle over my head.

"You made me do this and now when I need you you're gone. It's all your goddamn fault! I was fine before you got here!" I am the crazy person yelling at himself while walking down the street. Covered in soiled clothes and open wounds. Staggering and screaming. "You said you were here to help me." I whisper. "Help me!" I shout.

An intersection comes into sight at the end of the road. Black vehicles stretch from curb to curb.

"Shit."

"Here!" a black uniforms yells from behind a vehicle. Several agents take aim with their long-barrel rifles. At least twenty of them there, as though stacked on top of each other. Of course they'd close the road. Probably cleared out the entire neighborhood. I put my hands up like it'll help.

I hear a buzz and feel a pinch in my chest. It's like a giant mosquito bite. Another hit. Tranquilizer darts. Tubes with measurements like a syringe. A third hits my stomach. I start to see things . . . fuzzy. Supposed to take . . . three to ten minutes to work . . . depending on the weight of the animal. I'm the animal.

I mutter something I don't understand to the voice that doesn't exist in my head.

At least my hands don't hurt anymore. Or the stitches in my face. Or my leg. So that's kinda nice. Oop—asphalt is not soft. Probably not a good idea to lie in the road. Might get hit by a car. Or, like . . . a kid on a bicycle. Or a dog . . . on a bicycle. What would bicycles look like if we had four legs? That'd be funny. Guess is good a place as any a lie down. A leas dun't hurt . . . anymore . . . An' is quiet.

A' leas'—

9

"DON'T WORRY," SAYS THE VOICE FLOATING LISTLESSLY about in the air.

I open my eyes to see a more vivid sky than I remember seeing in a long time. Wispy clouds blow through the scene above me, rimmed on all sides like a clearing of canopy trees, separate from each other but forming into one solid mass topped by a sky I can see but can never reach. The darkness rises up from the ground. At my side is the ponytailed medic, kneeling down among the agents that surround me on all sides. Their gear is an inky black as though they'd been dipped head first in oil. They look down on me, some with tasers drawn. This is the only way our chase could possibly end. I see myself in the plastic over their faces. I'm lying in the road with my feet together and my arms out, face up to the bright sky above us all.

"The sedative is designed to dissolve after about an hour with no side effects," the medic says. She places one knee across my forearm. I don't feel her at all. "It's like an extremely concentrated cold medicine." She glances to the side. Her eyes are shining emeralds. "You may feel a little loopy afterwards, but that'll pass soon." Her other foot leans on my fingertips. Red spots cover her white gloves. She grits her teeth in concentration and takes a set of tweezers into the open wounds on my hand. On the other hand is a clean bandage. "At least you can't feel this," she says, dropping a tiny glass shard onto a blood-streaked cloth on the road.

I try to speak but nothing comes out.

"How's he doing?" says Choi in his measured

tone. A few agents part to allow him into the gathering around me.

"Cut himself up nicely, but should feel fine once I remove these slivers."

"How long until we can move him?"

"Not long," she replies. Her tongue peeks from the corner of her mouth as she tweezes out another glass splinter. "How's his eye?" she asks.

Choi kneels down over me. I see him straight ahead and in the reflection of the face shields all around. "Looks okay," he says. The freckles on his upper cheeks are distant suns and his eyes are leather brown.

"Odin," he says. I'm really starting to hate my name. At least the condescending way he says it. "I'm sorry." I'm starting to hate that word too. "I wish things didn't happen this way. It was never my intention, nor that of Project Solar Flare, that you be brought in like this." His face hangs big and detached from everything else. "We hoped that you'd understand and choose to join us in our work. It really is quite remarkable."

"You said you were going to help me," I mumbled, but not to Choi.

"We are, Odin. You may not believe me, but we are."

"Got it," says the medic in quiet triumph.

"I'm sure you'll understand eventually." Choi pushes to stand. "Finished?"

"Just need to dress it."

"All right," Choi says to me. His face looks short and fat from down here. "Remain calm and get some rest. We'll talk soon."

The agents clear a path for him to leave.

The gap between the agents is like a window into a different world. The blue above me fades to darkness. The wispy clouds become the dust of distant stars. The black-clad agents are mighty columns rising to the very edge of the black sky. Their faces are dotted lights. The medic at my side is a little girl clothed up to her chin. Her eyes are big and shallow and filled with sympathy. Then everything goes black.

———⌄———

It's the shaking that awakens me. The shaking and the slight rattle of metal on metal. The sky is replaced with a van ceiling. The agents are still around, although there are fewer and they are seated along the walls with me on a stretcher between them. The straps keep my head, hands, and legs in place. All I can move is my eyes. All I can see is the gray ceiling and the heads of the agents above me.

Their helmets are pulled off. They look like kids, just a little older than I am. They try not to look at me on the floor, but I catch one at my side glancing and immediately looking away. He takes on the dead-eye stare of the others. His short hair is matted down in places and mussed up in others.

I hear the hum of the motor vibrating the floor and a police siren in the space ahead of us.

"Sir," says the one I caught looking. "He's awake."

My chest just off the left shoulder itches where the first dart hit. My stomach under the end of the bottom rib on the right itches too, the second hit. The third as well, above my belly button. I really want to scratch them, but when I move, I feel the restraints dig into my hands and arms. I hear springs creak and leather squeak from the seat in front of me.

"Feeling better?" says Choi from somewhere above my head. I stretch to see him but can't move very far. "How much farther?" he says to someone who clearly isn't me.

"ETA seventeen minutes, sir."

"Make sure they're ready for the handoff."

"Yes sir."

I try to speak, but what comes out is, "Ahnidurashmahest."

"You know there was no other choice, right?"

I guess Choi is talking to me again. I really, really wish I could scratch my chest.

"The outside was no longer an option. Not because of you. Because of everyone else."

Itchy is the only feeling. No more pain, just itching. The other spots itch too, but the chest, that must be scratched. Must be.

"I hope you know that no one involved in this operation had any intention of hurting you. You're too valuable to risk. That's why we reacted as we did. Once it was clear that you could be hurt, it was obvious we needed to act. For your safety."

Nothing exists except the need to scratch.

"I'm glad we didn't have to, but we would have torn the entire town apart. That's how important you are. That's what I was trying to tell you before you decided to run."

He pauses for a second and I don't know why. What I do know is that one day my hands will be free and I'm gonna scratch the hell out of my chest and side and stomach and it's gonna feel awesome.

"This is why we chose to let you grow on your own, so that this day would never come. Let you decide for yourself rather than force you to join." He pauses again, probably considering what to say next. "Maybe we were too idealistic," he says. "We knew you'd figure it out eventually, but we hoped, or maybe assumed, that you'd see that our way was better for everyone. We thought that you'd reason it was best for the act to continue as long as necessary. That's when we'd approach and you'd see the good."

He exhales loudly. "Teenagers I guess, right?" He chuckles a little. "Anyway, the drug should be almost completely out of your system by the time we reach the base. The straps will come off once we're inside the gates."

He stops talking then. The seat springs creak as he turns away.

"Uh," I say.

The springs creak again.

"Ehu," I say.

"What?"

"It . . . ch," I finally manage. "So . . . itchy."

The van doors open to a bewildering light. I imagine it's similar to the one people describe seeing before death. That feels appropriate.

My eyes take a few moments to adjust. We're inside what looks like a large hangar with four flood lights shining onto us. The agents around me with their helmets back on don't even seem to flinch from the brightness.

The agents at my sides help me out of the back of the van. My shackles clank on the van floor as I shuffle my feet forward. I have to sit in order to step to the ground. One of the agents at my side, the one I'd caught looking before, pulls me up by the arm. "You get used to them," he said. The shackles are better than the restraints. Another example of that "freedom" Choi told me about.

A second and better look at the room reveals soldiers lined along the interior walls both on the ground and on a catwalk about twenty feet up. They stand facing us with their machine guns in both hands crossing their bodies. They look like toys occupying some kid's shelf. The far wall has a large window in front of a room of computer monitors and three people who aren't wearing the desert combat gear that the soldiers are. The floor has long tracks from braking tires, oil stains around metal grates, and old and corroded barrels piled in the back in a gap between soldiers. The rounded ceiling has a grid of visible support beams. It's almost silly, how intimidating it all is. As though one gun couldn't do the job of the dozens ready to fire on me. Guess they haven't heard that I'm too valuable to harm.

I'm led around the front of the van to face the hangar entrance, an opening big enough to fit the wingspan of the largest plane I've ever seen with plenty of room to spare. The agents at my side pull me to the center of their wide line. In front of us, framed by the half-drawn metal gate behind them, is a very angular man with three stars on his uniform shoulders whom I recognize from Choi's memory.

Everything about General Delgado is stern: the cracks around his eyes and down his cheeks, the downward edges of his mouth, the little eyes staring from between jagged lines. His uniform looks as stiff as a science fair poster board. Even his hair is nothing but jagged points. Another dozen soldiers stand behind him in full combat gear. Gas grenades hang from their body armor, large scopes sit on top of their assault rifles, night vision goggles extend up from their helmets. All this just for me. Such praise.

Choi moves into position between myself and the general to make our sides exact duplicates of each other.

"Sir, package is secured for delivery," Choi says with none of his usual flourish.

"Sorry to see the doctor's little experiment in child psychology didn't work, Mr. Choi," Delgado says. There's a music to his tone, like the narrator of a nature documentary. "We'll take the package from here."

"Yes, General," Choi says.

I see a hint of regret in the way Choi avoids looking at me. He begins to step away before stopping. He leans closer while still avoiding eye contact. "Watch yourself," he whispers.

He nods to the agents at my sides before walking away. The chains tug on my ankles as we walk forward, the agents pulling me on, to only a few feet from the general. He looks to be at least half a foot taller than I am. He probably isn't. He only feels that way. He says nothing as the soldiers file out from behind him and encircle both of us. "Follow," he says.

"Like I have a choice," I mutter, "ever."

The metal jingles with my every short step. I have to hustle to keep up with the rest of the group. The soldiers spread out around me, six behind and six in front, staggered from each other. It gives them each a clean line of fire. Delgado strides along at the front of the pack some fifteen feet ahead.

Late afternoon shadows creep across the runways with their reflectors and painted lines. Small patches of grass separate the different lanes. In the distance are other hangars and smaller structures, all of them closed. The only people in sight are those around me, with their long shadows stretching beyond my own. I can't believe that only a few hours ago I was sitting in front of an empty classroom talking to the principal of my high school and now I'm here, shackled and surrounded by a dozen heavily armed infantry soldiers and being led to who knows where. We couldn't have traveled that far.

Fort Colton, about two hours to the west and slightly south of my neighborhood. The lake would be somewhere north of here. We came to this base once for an air show when I was very small. The Blue Angels flew overhead in a tight V-formation. Fighter jets screamed through big loops and rolls in the sky, passing within feet of each other at unimaginable speeds. My favorite was an old biplane that climbed until the engine sputtered out. It dropped and went into a spin while pouring red and blue smoke from its wings. We got ice cream afterwards and I mentioned that my chocolate-vanilla swirl was like the smoke from that old plane. It was probably more of Aida and Ben's conditioning at work.

We approach a divided metal gate set into a concrete wall so smooth it looks brand new. Towers with spotlights line the top of the wall as armed guards patrol across it like those at a prison or a medieval castle. Within the walls is a short and squat structure of only two floors. A lattice of thick bars cover the nine symmetrically arranged windows across the building front. One wide door breaks up the arrangement. A small computer screen is embedded in the wall next to the door and a metal plate above the door reads *DHSDRDI142-01*.

"Stop," orders one of the soldiers behind me. Again, like I have a damn choice.

Delgado looks up to the top of the door. I barely see the reflection of glass up there, likely a camera behind it. The display screen shows a keypad like that of a smartphone. Oh, my phone! I wag my leg slightly to see if the phone shifts in my pocket. Nothing. Figures. My bag is gone too. So much for having something to read while I'm . . . wherever I'm going.

The doors seem to exhale as they slide open. They're at least a foot thick and have ridged bolts to lock them in place. The soldiers converge around me before we step in. Delgado turns.

"I don't have to tell you what happens if you present even the slightest hint of threat." He speaks with a growled menace that belies his otherwise soothing timbre. "The scientists might think you're some kind of hope, but to me you're nothing more than a bomb."

"I believe I'm entitled to a phone call at least," I say.

"Not here."

He turns back and starts through the door.

I try not to bump into the soldiers as we walk, but I still do. I hope it doesn't come off as a threat.

The soldiers around me make it difficult to see anything other than the upper walls and the rows of fluorescent lighting overhead. Every visible surface of the building smooth, likely plaster over concrete or steel. Fixtures are molded into the walls instead of attached to the surface. The seams are invisible. They cast no shadows. It's all white or light gray, making the lights overhead that much brighter.

I can smell the sweat of the soldiers around me, the oil on their guns. Their stomps are surprisingly light in the central corridor. I've gotten so accustomed to the noise of my chains that they're barely noticeable now. For a second, I catch a sliver of something between two of the soldiers, a break in the wall, a passage into another room. Metal bars separating it from this one. We continue on. Our tight grouping allows only the briefest glimpse of anything other than body armor, fatigues, and rifles.

The corridor ends with another pair of doors, an elevator. Delgado moves aside to let the soldiers pass. They herd me in, stopping and turning toward the front of the elevator in unison. My chains jingle as I rotate. The chains still rattle lightly after I face ahead, from my shaking. One of the soldiers at my side watches while I turn. Bloodshot spider webs cross the white of his eyeball. A large vein throbs just out of the mask over his face. I look away quickly as I shake even more. Delgado enters in front of us and the doors shut.

The elevator goes down for twenty-three seconds before stopping. I could calculate the distance if I knew the speed of descent. I don't. I don't know anything anymore. I can only guess that we're well below the base.

The doors open into a much larger passage. Ten feet, maybe twelve, wide enough that the soldiers no longer press against me as we exit the elevator. There's the murmur of people, the echo of footsteps, and the slamming of doors. It's like the hall at school, only narrower and without the cracks and chipped paint on the walls and ceiling, and with cameras set behind glass at regular intervals.

We continue on. In the wider gaps between soldiers, I see passages branching off this one. A pair of men in collared shirts and slacks wearing credentials around their necks stop their approach to our corridor. They turn away.

"Is this M.I.T.?" I ask.

"The package will be silent," Delgado replies, "or be silenced."

I hear the rattle of weapons shifting at my side.

We continue on past another intersection of branching halls and through an open area that resembles a waiting room. There's what appears to be a schedule under an embedded glass frame.

Several paces to my right is a heavy door with another keypad set in the wall. We continue forward, through another pair of foot-thick doors, and then another, until I can finally see the end of the hall.

Steel doors line the passage around us. Six on each side, separated by only a few feet. At the bottom of each door is a small flap, like a dog door for roadkill, with a lock next to it.

The soldiers turn as though they are limbs on the same massive body. Gears crank and the door now in front of us slowly opens. The soldiers in front of me turn to face me directly. The movement is terrifying. They don't look at me. My chains. One of them tugs harshly at my arms while undoing one lock and another kneels to unshackle my feet. The chains drop with a cacophonous thud. The soldiers in front sweep themselves and chains away in one motion while the soldiers behind push me forward into the small cell opened ahead. The door is already cranking closed before I turn. The soldiers stare, expressionless and indifferent, until they disappear.

A small bed in the corner, a sink attached to the top of what looks like a box with a hole in it and a roll of toilet paper in another corner, and that's all. The bed sheets are white and thin and folded onto the shallow mattress next to a foam pillow and a folded orange prison uniform. The uniform is a shock of color against the white of the room. Under the bed are a pair of black slippers.

A glass panel covers a camera in the same corner as the toilet. Privacy. How considerate. There are the same in-set lights along each wall, a small speaker in the exact center of the ceiling and four vents in each corner. Perhaps the vents are to keep a steady flow of air so the room doesn't become too stale, too cold, or too hot. Perhaps they're also to pump gas so I don't get too brave.

10

I TAKE A MOMENT TO GATHER MYSELF BEFORE THE anger begins.

I stomp around between the walls. Every surface is impossibly smooth. Seamless. Nothing to grip to or pull against. Nothing to focus on. No one to focus on. Choi is still too unclear in my head. Delgado even more so. The soldiers are all anonymous. Maybe that's why they wear the masks. I doubt even Aida and Ben know anything about what's happening or where I am. That would make the fight at the school far too calculated. No possible way David and those goons would have been in on this. Same with Brent and the others, Hauser and Faria, not a chance. I should get used to being without them. Without anyone. Never thought I'd actually miss Wendell's constant badgering.

I pace back and forth like a lion in a cage. The blank walls are perfect copies of each other. Only the stuff in front of them changes. "Is this what you wanted?" I say aloud, knowing there won't be a response. "Is this what I'm meant for?" I push against door. There is no give, no vibration, no echo. "Is this what 'comes next'? One of those 'important steps'? Huh?" I punch the door. My hand aches. I don't care. I bang my palms against the door until they ache too much to move. Red dots appear on the bandage over my wounds like inkblot tests. I kick the door instead.

I turn to the tinted glass over the camera in the corner. "Well?" I yell at whoever's watching on the other side. I look at the speaker in the middle of the ceiling and wait for a reply. "Hello?" I shout when only silence follows.

The pains and aches have returned while the

itching has disappeared. Kinda sad I never got the satisfaction of scratching. I feel the stitches in my face again, especially when my cheeks pull back to yell as I kick the door one more time. There's still an ache in my ribs and legs. The hands are the worst. I can't even bend my fingers. It was dumb to hit the door like that. It was dumb to even run. Not like it made any difference. I was always going to end up here between these smooth goddamn walls. This was their plan. Like Wendell said. Wendell, he led me to this place. Maybe he's involved somehow. Maybe he's not a voice at all but a chip implanted into my head to whisper ideas that would eventually lead me here. The black helicopters were real too. At least one of them.

Each of the bed's legs are welded into the floor. The base of the toilet and sink too. I can't lift them. Can't break them apart. The seams in the door are too narrow to picture how it works. Probably has locks in place to keep me from pushing. It's like they made this cell just for me. All part of their goddamn plan.

"You knew this didn't you?" I say to my absentee imagination. "Led me right here."

The orange uniform is the only bit of color I see outside of my own blood-soaked clothing. Even with the brownish stains and drops, I'd rather wear these clothes than that thing. Changing would mean giving up. It would be offering the last of my independent identity and becoming what they, *they*, want me to be. The bright orange prison uniform, the modern equivalent of the red "A" on the chest or the Star of David on the sleeve. Meant to mark me as other, as less than. I am anything but less than.

I pick the entire stack of orange clothes up in one bandaged hand. I march it over to the camera. I hold it up so they can get a good look at it. Then I crumple it and stuff it into the boxy toilet bowl. I hope their angle lets them see that.

I stomp around the room again. Seamless. I

want to continue pounding the walls but know it'll mean nothing. Plus my hands hurt too much to continue. I want to reach into the head of someone I know but that won't mean anything either. They probably aren't even aware that I've been taken. What are they going to think when I don't show up again? When David and Eric and Dylan and them return with their limbs in thick casts? No rumors they imagine will possibly be stranger than the truth I'm living. What would be the point? Not like they matter anymore. No matter. Not worth the energy.

A camera means there's at least one person watching. Could be a bunch of them. Delgado and all his guys standing around a monitor laughing as I futilely destroy myself even more. "I bet you're enjoying this," I say to the glass in the corner. "Watching me in here. For all I know you're some kind of perv that gets off on this kind of thing. Teenage boys in little boxes." I flick my wrist to lift one of the black slippers from the floor and shoot it at the camera. It bounces uselessly off the glass and drops onto the uniform in the toilet. I race to the front of the camera. My stitches sting as I scream, "What do you want?" I wipe a trickle of blood from between the threads. Another bad idea, like pounding my hands bloody. Bloodier.

"You did this," I whisper. "You led me here. Not them. You. You took my life away. And then you ran off. Somewhere else. Whatever the fuck that is. Stay there. You were probably never even real in the first place. You were—"

"Odin."

My name through the speaker. Not in my head. I look at the camera.

"Hello, son."

"Dad?" I say toward the glass.

"We can't hear you on this side," Ben says. A mechanical hiss underlines his voice. "Looks like you can hear us."

I look to the camera and nod.

"Good."

"Hi, Odin," Aida says. "Are you hurt?"

I glare at the camera and hold my palms up to them. Let them see the drops of blood leaking through the bandages.

"Should we ask for a doctor?"

I turn away from the camera to sit on the bed. The mattress is thin but surprisingly firm and pleasant.

Enough silence follows that I watch the door as though the gears would begin to grind open and either Ben or Aida or both will miraculously materialize into the room in front of me. No. They're in a monitor room. Several troops in casual gear sit at consoles in front of many screens each. Must be one for every camera in the entire complex. Ben and Aida stand behind one soldier with only twelve screens. Each screen is an identical image except one, me. I see myself looking up at the camera in the corner. A blank look on my face. Not like the scowl from a moment ago.

"Just a couple of minutes please," Ben says to an officer. "Father to son."

"Two minutes," the officer says. He gestures for the monitors to leave. They place their headsets down and march out quietly. "Press number four when you're ready to speak."

"Thank you."

"Thanks," says Aida.

The door closes behind them.

Ben picks the headset up from the console. He surveys the complex series of buttons and switches until finding the "4" button positioned under the screen. The buttons resemble the "on air" lights of old radio stations. They both stare into the monitor where I appear blank, staring at the floor in front of the cell bed as though I'm light years away. I faintly hear, "There we go," in my room a second before I see Ben speak.

"There we go," he says, "we asked for a bit more privacy."

Every word enters my mind twice, one second apart, like an extremely deep echo.

Ben motions for Aida to sit in the chair in front

of the console. He places his hand on her shoulder. A window in the monitor room overlooks a wide expanse in which several mechanics are stripping out the wires from old computer monitors. A huge, lifting door occupies the entire wall behind the mechanics. The area appears to branch far beyond the limits of the window with piles of scrap accumulating against the walls.

"We came as soon as we were able to," he says. Aida's eyes close. Ben doesn't see this. "Honestly there's so much I'd like to say right now. I guess the most important thing is that I'm sorry for everything that's happened."

Aida buries her face in her hands. I remain distant on the screen.

"I can't help thinking that if we had done a better job, then you wouldn't be here."

That's when Aida starts sobbing.

"At least not in this way." Ben wipes his eyes and looks down at Aida. "I guess we failed you." He rubs her shoulder. "You trusted us and we let you down." It's the closest my father has come to crying since his own father died.

He glances at the monitor. I remain still as death. "You must hate us for lying."

It's not comfortable watching the past play out in real time instead of the usual blur of thought. It's slow and uncertain. Feels like I should be able to change what comes next.

"They told us custody is for your own safety. I'm not sure I believe that anymore." He sniffs as a tear falls off his face. "Whether or not you believe us ever again, we want you to know that we are so proud of you." His voice breaks up as he finishes the sentence. Aida drops her hands from her face. She stares at the floor in the same way I do. Ben continues, "We are proud of who you are, not because of us, but because of yourself. And we'll be proud of what you will become."

And what is that? I want to ask.

"You're our son," he says, "since the day we met. You always will be our son." He's struggling now. "And we are so privileged to have been a part of your life." He pats Aida's shoulder twice before removing the headset and handing it down to her. His face cracks into a thousand pieces as the tears fall.

There is a moment of silence.

I should move. I should give them some indication that I can hear them.

Aida inhales deeply before speaking.

"Odin, I just want to tell you, none of what happened is your fault," she says. "We just . . . no one knows how to handle someone as extraordinary as you. They're scared and they don't know what's going to happen. They react with fear because that's all they know." She continues to stare at the floor. "God, what am I going to tell Andre?" she says more to herself than me. "He'll never understand," she whispers. "He's looks up to you so much."

Really?

There's a knock on the monitor room door. The sound snaps Ben immediately into order. He taps

Aida's shoulder again and motions for the headset. She gives it up freely.

"We need to go now, son," he says in a very composed manner. He places both of his hands on both of her shoulders. "We'll try to visit you as soon as we're able." He reaches to the lit-up button on the console. "Hang in there," he says. "We love you."

The button goes dark.

It could be more conditioning. They could be using my connection to them to guilt me into going along with whatever Delgado has planned. They want me feel it all: guilt, regret, responsibility. Their manipulation. It works.

My room is silent again. Silent and small and empty. So empty.

Dinner is a sort of . . . stew . . . that's almost more gray than brown and with a uniformly mushy texture. Parts of it tastes slightly of either overly tender beef or soft carrot. It came through the flap at the bottom of the door on a plastic tray with a plastic spoon and an order: "You have fifteen minutes to eat." It's about the same size as the trays in the lunch room at school except with one compartment for food instead of four. At least school gave us an hour to finish. I eat every bite of the food with no idea what time it is or when I'll be fed again. I slide the tray and spoon back out. The flap snaps into place on the door as though vacuumed to it. I hear the key locking the only hole in the door and then nothing else.

I sit on the bed and stare at the wall. A blank, white wall, like one of the dry erase boards at school without the stray marks left from previous classes, or the other students trying not to get caught whispering, or the teachers telling those students to please pay attention because what's on the board now will be on the test later. So this blank wall is nothing like those boards. Everyone in class knows that our time spent staring at white boards will eventually end. We'll move onto a new class with a different board. We'll have a break between classes. Lunch. Weekends. Holidays. Finally, graduation. The best thing about high school is that it's temporary. There's comfort in knowing that however long it may feel, high school does, in fact, end. Here, with this blank white wall, there is no such promise. There's just a blank wall. Until the lights go off. Then there's just slightly varying shades of black.

The camera probably has a night setting, that bizarre green-lit negative function like in war movies, so they can watch me all the time. Watched all the time. I should be used to that by now. Guess the lights off is their way of telling me to sleep. At least at home, "home," they allowed me enough freedom to decide that for myself.

I take my shoes and socks off mostly to keep them from smelling too bad. The floor makes my feet only slightly cooler. I imagine at some point I'll be allowed to shower. The orange uniform remains soaking in the toilet. I look from the toilet-soaked prison uniform to the camera and back. Then I give them the finger. I won't become what they want me to. Let their night vision soak that in.

The pillow is so thin it may as well not be there. The room isn't hot or cold but I pull the scratchy sheet on anyway. I slip off my shirt and pants. May as well keep them fresh for as long as possible, blood stains and all. My only set of clothes. Not *theirs*. In the dark I can barely see the stains on the bandages over my hands. "Can you see this?" I ask. "See what's happened because of you?"

I feel the stretch as I look down to check the bruise on my ribs. Invisible in the dark. I poke at it and wince. Painful but probably not broken. I pull my knee up and contort under the sheet to see it. The bruise there is smaller and directly on the bone. Also not broken. I lie flat and try not to think of the pain.

It's weird knowing that Ben and Aida aren't on

the other side of the house, Andre on the other side of the hall. Last night, my last night, Mom made a chicken Caesar salad. Dad joked that she was trying to make us all into rabbits. Andre held a lettuce leaf in both hands to take tiny bites. Mom tried not to show frustration because then Dad would win. I wish I'd done something at the time. Laughed or smiled at them, even if it was fake.

Brent didn't have much of a choice either. He wouldn't have had any chance against Eric, let alone the rest of them. I don't think he's ever been a fight that didn't involve either words or controllers. Everyone likes him too much anyway. Brent told me he had been interested in Evelyn during freshman year. Then he met Heidi and they dated for a while. He forgot about Evelyn with Heidi and said he lost all interest when he and I became friends because you don't make a move on the girl your friend likes. I wonder if that still applies now, since we're not really friends. He'd probably be better with her than most of the other guys. I mean, since it doesn't look like I have any chance. Still not fun to think about.

They did talk about me, Brent and Evelyn. He wasn't lying about that. She walked up to him at his locker about three weeks ago, a week after neither of them showed up for my party, and asked if he'd spoken to me.

"No," Brent said, shaking his head. "Not since his birthday."

"Oh right, how was that?"

"I don't know," he said.

"You didn't go either?"

He finished changing his books and closed the locker.

"You think that's why he's been so quiet?" Evelyn asked.

"I have no ideas about him anymore."

"Yeah."

It was just under two weeks later that they spoke again for more than passing greetings, a Thursday, the day after I was first sent to the office for "acting smart" in Mr. Zeller's class. She was there, she saw it all.

"Did you hear about Odin?" she asked him while he was sitting at the junior benches waiting for school to begin.

"No," he said, "we don't talk anymore."

"He started acting really strange during physics yesterday. He was like guessing which questions would have which answers on the test and stuff. Zeller got so pissed."

"Man," Brent said, looking at the ground, shaking his head.

"He doesn't talk to me anymore, either," Evelyn said. "You think he hates me for flaking on his party like that? I wanted to go but, you know, it was really weird that day."

"Yeah," Brent said. "Oh, I mean about it being weird, not about him hating you. I don't think Odin can really hate people. Or, I thought he couldn't."

Evelyn looked around, at the benches and the

space immediately surrounding them. "I saw it," she said. "I was right over there," she pointed to where she was standing during the fight, slightly back from the benches and still on the path away from the school. Her voice went quieter. "It was actually kinda badass the way he stood up to all of them."

"No one ever told me what he actually said."

"I don't really know. It was pretty quiet and I was kinda scared for him. But it was like he finally didn't care what people thought. It was cool. Until . . ."

"Yeah."

"Well, if you do talk to him, tell him I'm sorry and he should call me or something."

Brent nodded.

He was a good guy. Really he was. I shouldn't have shut him out like that. Maybe if I didn't, then he would have given me some warning about David. Shutting everyone out only let them create their own reality about me. Not Brent and Evelyn in particular, but the others, Eric and Dylan and those guys. I did the same thing with my parents. The little voice in my head built its own reality, furthered by my imagination and uncertain and resentment. I built them into devious monsters when in reality . . . they weren't. Not malicious ones. "Comes back. Starts a fucking mess. And then—poof—he's gone," I say aloud. They're all gone.

I roll onto my uninjured side and pull the sheet over my face. The camera probably has a night vision setting. There may be several soldiers watching. I don't want them to see me cry.

───────⌣───────

Breakfast: a sort of thick, milky concoction that looks like an omelet filled with oatmeal and then run through a blender. I drink warm water from the faucet. A small toothbrush and clear container of toothpaste comes with the meal. Half of the toothbrush handle breaks the first time I used it. The guard demands I return the broken piece.

Lunch: half a potato cut into eight pieces. Uncooked.

Dinner: a thick reddish sauce with diced bits of what could be either abnormally large beans or potato chucks and long strains of a soggy green plant. I wish it was more like Mom's rabbit food.

Breakfast: blended omelet-oatmeal, this time with pieces of something, possibly apple peel.

Lunch: the other half of the potato.

Dinner: more of the gray-brown pseudo-stew. I guess it was leftovers day.

Breakfast: it's chucky and slightly gelatinous.

Lunch: raw starch.

Dinner: who cares just eat it. Not like there's anything better to do.

Breakfast: . . .

Lunch: Yay . . . stuff!

Dinner: Has become something to look forward

to. I never know what it's going to be, even after eating it, and that makes it exciting.

Meals have replaced classes in how I tell what time it is. Lights on is the morning bell. Lights out is bedtime. Between lights on and lights out I sit and stare at the walls. Gym is pacing back and forth and doing push-ups and sit-ups on the floor. Art is tearing the orange prison clothes into little strips of color. English is re-reading old books in my head. Physics is trying to find cracks in the walls. History is watching my friends and family. Math is trying to calculate how long I've been here.

The calendar on Mom's desk says it's Thursday, a full week since my arrival. She has a meeting at eleven o'clock with Ma's Kitchen Catering for a breast cancer fundraiser next month.

Dad was told six days ago by his superiors not to ask about me. I am no longer their responsibility. He asked if they could come visit and was told that when visitation is possible, he will be informed. He didn't ask again.

Mom and Dad sent Andre to the Aukermans' house the night they came to see me after my fight. Fights. They requested he not be allowed to watch television until they came to pick him up. Mr. Aukerman let him play video games in his chair with the built-in speakers. They ate dinner and only after Mom and Dad picked him up did he wonder where they went. They said I'd been invited to stay at UW for a week as part of a special recruitment for students that do exceptionally well at school.

"What about finals?" Andre asked as he picked cat hair off his clothes.

"He'll still go to school," Mom said, "he's just staying in the dorm to see how it feels." Andre believed that. He asked if he'd be able to do the same thing when he got older. They haven't yet decided what to say tonight when my stay is supposedly over. They've either said nothing or cried, every night, as soon as Andre goes to his room to sleep.

Brent faked being sick the whole week to keep from having to go to school. He called Richard on

Tuesday. Richard was surprised Brent hadn't heard that I'd disappeared while David, Eric, and Dylan were in the hospital. T.J. and Ross were hurt too, but not badly. Weird thing is that neither of them said anything about what happened.

The lunchroom benches were straightened almost immediately after I was caught. Hauser's office window and chair were fixed. The glass cleaned up. The concrete step where David punched me and the door I was pulled through were spotless. The news that night was of a gas leak forcing the school and the neighborhood to be temporarily evacuated. Finals are still scheduled for next week, even if a handful of students are out with unexplained injuries or illnesses.

Maria heard from Janice that I was expelled from school for misbehaving in class. Alison thought that was so badass. Stephanie said that she overheard Ms. O'Hara in the office tell Mr. Ferguson, the guidance counselor, that I was in a coma in the hospital and that's why Ross and T.J. are refusing to say anything about what happened. Alison didn't believe that one bit. Lori said that Trent told her that Lonnie heard that I was refusing to come back to school until the vending machines brought back the sodas. Alison thought that was stupid. Evelyn got up and left. She hasn't spoken to anyone about me at all. Not even Brent. She sent messages to my phone. *Are you okay? What happened? Where are you? I wish you would talk to me.* The last one read, *I'm sorry.*

This is why bland, unremarkable slop is the highlight of my day. It's better than watching my family and friends struggle to find some reason why I'm not there, which is better than staring at smooth walls with no way out. Not even for me. Now I talk to myself despite knowing the answer will be nothing all the time.

The grind of the door gears is deafening in how it breaks the silence. The door takes forever to pull away from the frame. In the growing gap, I see patches of dark to light brown, pouches, armor, guns. I haven't showered in a week. I've only changed these clothes to take them off at night. I brush with the little bristle head and wash my face every morning, mindful of the stitches. The door opens to soldiers three wide and three deep. Desert combat gloves, kneepads, pouch-covered vests, and rifles angle down. Only their helmets are missing from a potential war zone. Nothing moves but their eyes, darting round to the room. Not like the monitor room won't tell them what to expect over the communication sets they all wear. I hear feet shuffling over the concrete floor. Shadows move from the second row of soldiers. The three in the front slide over.

She's smaller than I remember, but I was smaller then too. Her hair is grayer. The lines on her forehead are more pronounced and her chin has started to sag. In other ways, she looks exactly the same.

The images spring effortlessly to mind. The way

her eyebrows lifted whenever she spoke, regardless of what she said. Her cheeks puffed as though filled with cotton balls when she laughed. She leaned on one arm in her chair with the other arm stretched out, her legs crossed, and facing an angle so when she spoke only her face and one hand would be turned toward me.

She steps into the cell and sniffs the air. "My god," she says, "when was the last time you bathed?"

"Dr. Burnett?" I say.

"And those clothes." The blood stains have turned a crusty brown. "Why didn't you just change?"

She looks at the pile of orange strips left in the corner.

"Oh . . . well, come on," she says, waving for me to step forward. "We have an appointment."

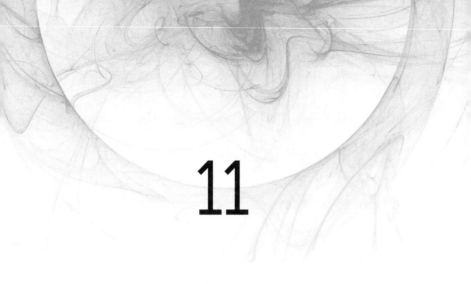

11

"**H**ow is it?" Dr. Burnett asks about the ham-burger and French fries on the plate in front of me.

I nod while chewing greedily. I'm not much of a burger and fries eater, and honestly the meal is rather unremarkable, but for now this burger is the single greatest thing I have ever eaten in my entire life.

"Much better than the slop in your cell, right?" Her eyebrows still rise when she speaks.

I swallow quickly.

"I have no idea what that stuff is either," she says before I can ask the question.

We sit in the middle of a small mess hall with

several tables and cushioned chairs and a high ceiling. It's still all white, but that's forgivable when there's a window to a kitchen where a cook makes one of three lunch choices upon request and numerous hallways lead in every direction with the sounds of people walking and talking and the hum of machines lingering quietly in the background. You never miss ambient noise until it's gone. Total silence is quite disturbing. It sounds like something has gone horribly wrong.

"Much better," she says again, a certain trepidation in her voice.

The soldiers surrounded me immediately as I stepped out of my cell. We marched through the narrow hall and the waiting room with the large door that I saw on my way in. We continued toward the elevator before turning left into another hallway.

Every corridor looks the same through a wall of

camouflage and guns until the soldiers parted at a door with a small sign next to it reading: *Shower*. From behind, my escort, Dr. Burnett, shouted, "You have ten minutes to wash that stink off."

The water wasn't very hot but I still wanted to stay under it forever. When I exited my clothes were gone with just an orange uniform and black slippers left in their place. One way or another, they would make me play my part.

From there we marched to the infirmary where my stitches were removed. The removal stung but felt better coming out than going in. My nearly-healed hands were wrapped in fresh bandages and my leg and ribs were both checked. The bruises were already disappearing; in fact, everything was healing nicely.

Now it's the cafeteria. The greatest place in the world. She ordered the meal for me and sat mostly silent as I devoured half of the burger in one bite. Only two bites and a whole mess of fries remain. Then there's the big glass or whatever the hell the bubbly brown liquid it is. I don't care. It's better than lukewarm water that's simultaneously both thin and oily. It will all be consumed.

"Odin," she says to pull my attention, "I'm incredibly sorry for everything that's happened."

"Sorry. Everyone's so sorry," I say. "It's like a chorus. Doesn't change anything."

"I understand. I wish this was . . ." She looks around the room. Guards line each of the walls between the exits. She leans both of her elbows on the table, folding one arm over the other.

"I promise things will get better now. If you want them to. Odin," she taps the table so that I look at her. "Do you understand what I'm saying?" She keeps her elbows on the table. She uses her left hand to rub behind her right ear three times and then stops. I don't remember her making a motion like that before.

I nod.

"Good." She looks around again. The mess hall, like the rest of the facility as I've seen it so far, is spotless, with lights and cameras built into the plaster-covered concrete. Even the lunch menu is embedded behind glass. We're underground, yet the air is fresher here than in most of my classrooms.

"This whole building exists because of you," she says. "It's here to help us learn about you. Help you learn about yourself. Then, hopefully, learn what we can do together to help the rest of the world."

I tilt my head at this. She looks over my shoulder, at the soldiers again.

"Our goal here is knowledge. We have some theories but can't be sure this knowledge will lead to anything practical. Most scientific breakthroughs start that way. No determined goal. One day you're growing mold in a Petri dish and the next day you're creating the world's first antibiotic. That's the fun part," she says with a puffy smile, "not knowing."

Her smile disappears when our eyes meet. There is fear in them. Then the smile returns.

"We hope that you'll be willing to help us with this."

I pick up a fry. It's warm and crunchy and so much better cooked than raw.

"If you don't mind, Odin" she says, emphasizing my name so that I'll look at her. She raises her hand to rub behind her ear again. Three times and then down. "I'd like to ask you a couple of questions to help direct our research."

I nod while shoving another fry in my mouth. She didn't used to talk this way, so stilted and vague. She was always much more direct. Kind but not cloying. She wants me to notice something.

"When you use one of your abilities, how does it feel?"

I shrug. "Nothing really. I just picture what I'd like to have happen and it kinda happens."

"Anything?" she asks.

"Not anything, but it's getting easier." I start

to float one of the fries from the plate. She places her hand over it. I let it drop. She waves her hand flatly to one side.

"And when you see things, what's that like?" There's the hand to the ear once again. Three rubs and down.

"It's like watching a movie, only it actually happened."

"Can you do this for anyone at any time?"

"I don't think so," I'm sure she knows this. Whether we talked about it before, years ago, or not. She must know this already. "They need to be in front of me or familiar enough that I can hold an image of them in my mind. Then I key in on one particular moment. In the same way as scanning a book for specific words."

"You can do this with, say, your friends? You can look into Brent or Richard or Wendell without problems?"

Wendell. She's the only one other than Kevin who knows. I never told Kevin his name.

"Yes," I say after finishing another fry. "Up until a few seconds in the past. Never the exact present."

"Where is Wendell now?" she asks, hand back to the ear. "Can you look for him?"

She's not asking about Wendell.

I imagine Dr. Burnett making that motion, elbows on a table with her left hand reaching across her chest to rub behind her right ear.

It was two days ago in an office, not the office I knew from when I was a kid, a different one with no windows and one door. She'd just gotten off a phone call with Director Braxton about me being taken into custody. I want to see everything but key in on that motion instead.

"Odin," she said, eyebrows up, "you need to listen to me." She spoke as though I were standing in front of her instead of the empty chair and the bare wall several feet away. "I'm sure you know what this is: the cleaning, the food, the medical attention, the friendly face returning after years away." In those moments of joy and uncertainty, I hadn't considered it, but it was obvious. They were building me up after breaking me down. Shameful I hadn't noticed it before, but then again, food.

"This is not anything even close to what I pictured for you when we instituted your development plan. You were to be given the best environment within reason. Raised as close to normally as possible, if such a thing as normal exists." That's more like the Dr. Burnett I knew. "Nothing too difficult but nothing so lavish as to distance you from the rest of humanity. You were supposed to see the good in people so that you would want to be good as well.

"The facility you're in now was built in the hope that you would join us in learning about what makes you special. What we learn from you could forever change our understanding of the universe and how we as humans exist in it. I always hoped that your natural curiosity and intelligence would entice you to help us."

She looked down at her desk, pausing for a moment, and then raised her eyebrows to continue.

"But it was also built for containment. Knowledge in and of itself isn't enough for most people. My boss, Braxton, you saw him through Randall's memory, is being constantly pressured by his military liaison, Delgado, to find a practical military use for our research. I'm confident you know what that means." Practical military use: better ways of killing people.

She paused and looked away again. She almost never did that during our sessions. She was always focused.

"I've been trying for years to prevent that. You can see all that if you wish, but time is short right now." She took a long breath. "Funding for pure research is hard to come by. Between war, bad economics, loss of revenue, aging population, there's little money in DHS for anything except border security and anti-terrorism operations. Without Pentagon support, we would have lost everything, including you. There were even some who regarded you as a potential threat and proposed that we . . ."

She shook her head.

"I'm getting off track. What happened before isn't important. How we proceed from here is. I know this is a bad situation. I know you'd rather be back to your old life, even if that was nothing more than a lie, although, hopefully a pleasant one." Her cheek ticks up in an attempt to smile. "But none of that is possible. Believe me, I wish it were. You need to make the best of this now. Our goal needs to be understanding how and why you're able to do the things you can. My theory is that if our research proves fruitful, we can negotiate a better situation for you. Until then, for your sake, for all of us: myself, Choi, our project, the curious everywhere, don't destroy all that we've worked for. Not this time. You have no idea how unique you are." She laughed slightly, once, her cheeks puffing. "None of us do, and that's the best part," she said with a smile, "not knowing." Then the smile disappeared. Her back straightened. "This is a dangerous place, Odin. Watch yourself."

"Now," she said, "tell me your friend Wendell is in his biology class studying the Hardy-Weinberg principle."

———⌄———

She sits quietly in front me, exactly the same, but in a different place. Soldiers line the wall behind her.

"He's in his biology class," I say. "They're studying the Hardy-Weinberg principle."

She nods. "Good." She glances over my shoulder.

I resume eating the last of the fries. They're colder, chewier, and less appealing than they were before.

"Anything else you'd like?" she asks when I take a last long swallow from the glass.

I shake my head. She nods.

She stands and signals to the soldiers behind me. I rise as well. The soldiers gather around us. We take the long, slow walk through the white hallways hidden behind the mass of captors. I hear the leather of the gun straps stretch with each of the soldiers' steps. These aren't dart or tranquilizer guns. There are no rubber bullets here. These are real. These are deadly.

We stop in front of my cell door. I hear the gears open the door. The soldiers with the real guns step aside. The orange strips are gone, a fresh uniform in their place. I take a breath and walk forward across the deep canal in the floor designed to divide me from everyone else. The door begins to close.

"We'll talk more tomorrow," Dr. Burnett says from behind the three soldiers blocking the exit. "Think about what I said." The gears go silent. All that's left are blank white walls and empty air.

I look up at the speaker in the ceiling, the grid of little holes on a white square in a larger white square on one side of a white cube. Over to the camera, a black box in a clear box in the corner of a white box. Then there's the single, isolated creature in the middle of it, bright orange, so he can be quickly identified. I am what they want me to be, where they want me to be, about to do what they want me to do. Not even the illusion of choice. This is how I live now.

See what happens when I leave you alone?